THE APACHE KID

Clay Fisher

First published in the UK by Mills and Boon

This hardback edition 2008
by BBC Audiobooks Ltd
by arrangement with
Golden West Literary Agency

ISBN 978 1 405 68230 5

British Library Cataloguing in Publication Data available.

Printed and bound in Great Britain by
CPI Antony Rowe, Chippenham, Wiltshire

For my brother, Bruce G. Allen

HISTORICAL NOTE

The San Carlos Apache Niño—called "Kid" by his white biographers—was a living fact of history. As such, he deserves to be weighed in the same scale of Southwestern importance with Cochise, Mangas Coloradas, Massai, Geronimo, Roman Nose or Quanah Parker. Yet so wild was he, so savage, wolflike and alone in his now classic eight-year duel to the death with the United States Cavalry, that no solitary detail of his personal life has come down in the Government records. It is to the folklore of his own Apache people that one must turn for the viable facts with which to fill in the silent breaks in the dusty trail of army reports, territorial records and contemporary newspaper accounts which compose the official documentation. But it is only from an interweaving of the two sources—the half-century-old Indian tales with the hard words of the white man's history—that there emerges the faint pattern of the whole truth and that one is able to see, fleetingly, both the lights and the shadows of the legend that was Niño, the Apache Kid.

C.F.

San Carlos Reservation
1960

Prologue

The young warrior was straight as the water reeds which grew along the Gila. He was strong as the rock of Old Chutanay, the tabletop mesa which stood beyond the river. The young woman upon whom his eyes waited and his heart dwelled was also straight and strong, but with that exciting softness reserved for her sex.

After enough time had gone by, the warrior led up his ponies and tied them before the wickiup of the young woman's father. He lay, then, the night through watching them and watching the doorway of the wickiup. When, at last, the turquoise daylight invaded the valley of the Gila, the woman drew aside the deerhide hangings of the door, untethered the animals and led them to drink at stream's edge.

The bargain struck, the lovers departed the *rancheria* of the girl's father to settle upon another part of the river. It was a lonely part where the Rio San Carlos came down to join the mother stream and where the land was a bake oven of heat. Why they came to such a desolate place is not easy to imagine. Perhaps they had a premonition of the evil to issue from them. Perhaps they chose the site precisely because it was what it appeared to be—the perfect harsh incubator and pitiless rearing pen for their savage offspring.

Whether by direction of this feral instinct or simply through some aimless Indian whim, the selection served its numbered purpose: the child was born there in 1869. Or a little before. Or a little after.

His father, some say, named him Red Wolf, although Red Wolf is not a typical Apache name and no document exists to support its use in this case. Like the date of his birth, the infant's name has not come down as an exact thing. Nor does it matter. He was, let us say, three or four or five years old, a button-eyed, bright and friendly little Indian boy, when General Howard and the Old Camp Grant garrison arrived upon the Gila from the San Pedro to establish the new reservation.

The Army's reason for selecting the San Carlos was by all odds more readily evident than that of the boy's parents. The naked rock of the desert thereabout was merely the fiercest hell of furnace heat available, making it the logical Government choice for improving the lot of nomad mountain Apaches from the high pine mesas of the Mogollons.

When the soldiers first came, little Red Wolf was the sole child, red or white, living within range of their barren encampment. He proved an instant, continuing hit with the lonely troopers, spending more time on the army post than at the *rancheria* of his father. In the words of one veteran cavalryman who remembered him particularly, "He knocked out his milk teeth on the barrel of my old Colt Dragoon and we, all of us, took turns drying his diaper spot with the handiest swatch of U.S. rifle patches."

By 1885, when the boy was sixteen, Al Seiber, Army Chief of enlisted Apache Scouts, enrolled him in Company F of this command, making him the youngest Indian ever to serve, by the record, in the regular U.S. forces.

There was reason for the distinction beyond strict considerations of the youth's popularity on the post. He had become the finest trailer in Arizona, possibly in the entire West. Other qualified opinions than Seiber's—Tom Horn's for one—agreed in this estimate. Yet, as an Apache, his larger notoriety continued to be his unparalleled position of trust with the tough soldiers of Camp

San Carlos. Again quoting the old cavalryman: "You could turn him loose with your kid sister and never miss a wink of sleep."

With year's end, 1886, climaxed by the September surrender of Geronimo in Skeleton Canyon, the entire number of Apache hostiles had been hunted down by the soldiers whom the San Carlos boy so admired and for whom, against his own people, he scouted so faithfully.

Cochise, Mangas Coloradas, Chatto, Chihuahua, Loco, Benito, Nache, all had been killed or captured. The list of vanquished Apache great was complete save for one name which had not yet been imagined to belong upon it. And which, as history unfolded in the swift years to come, gained a more evil reputation than any already delineated there. This last legend of Apache resistance, in fact, was destined never to be brought to earth. The warrior who created it disappeared as mysteriously as though he had vanished into a granite cliff. The U.S. Army today has no more idea what became of him than it did in those long-ago times when each rock in the Sierra Ancho hid a savage red fighting man. It doesn't even know his true given name. All it does know is the record of defeat which he inflicted upon it and the consuming hatred with which its cursing, sweat-caked troopers pursued him in the grim days when the least whisper of his nearness struck the fear of God into every white heart from Yuma to Las Cruces.

This is the story of that last Apache.

The one called Niño, the Apache Kid.

This is the way in which he earned his place with Cochise, Mangas Coloradas and Geronimo.

1

The five Indian horsemen sat their mounts looking down on the tent lights of San Carlos. The night was quiet as only the desert can be quiet. And it was beautiful. But in the breast of the Apache leader there was no quiet and no beauty.

"What do you say, Niño?" asked one of his companions. "You going down, or not?"

These were reservation Indians, speaking in English. Their leader answered in kind, the nature of his words reflecting the years of white influence.

"We'll wait a while," he said. "I want to think."

"All right," nodded the other, "think. But remember we came here to do something big."

Niño only moved his head. Another of his companions, however, spoke quickly.

"Yes, what's the matter?" he frowned. "You haven't done anything wrong. Old Rip killed your father, didn't he? And you had to kill Old Rip for that, didn't you? Now Seiber sends for you to quit hiding and to come in and talk it over with him and here you are hesitating as though it was you, instead of those soldiers, that was going to get hurt down there. I don't understand it. I think you're afraid."

"No," said Niño, "I'm not afraid. Otherwise, why am I here?"

"That's what we're beginning to wonder," said a third Indian. "Come on, let's go down and see Seiber. We're all scouts of his; he won't harm us."

Niño shook his head, looking down at the chevrons on his dark blue cavalry shirt.

"We're all scouts of his, yes," he said. "But I am the only sergeant. I was the one Seiber trusted. When he went to Camp Apache with Captain Pierce, it was me he left in charge of the scouts at San Carlos. Can I forget that? Can I forget that he trusted me and that I betrayed him?"

"You only obeyed Apache law," argued the first of his fellows. "You had to kill the murderer of your father."

Again Niño shook his head.

"Apache law says also that a man will die before he betrays his friend who trusts him," he murmured. "Thus I have kept the law on the right hand and broken it on the left. What am I to do?"

The last of his companions, a thin, lizard-dry Tonto Apache of middle age, spoke raspingly.

"Well, either kill yourself, or don't. But the others will be along soon and they aren't coming to sit up here on the mesa and watch the tent lights."

The "others" were a ragtag of renegade Apaches, refugees from other reservations, fugitives from San Carlos, fellow deserters from Seiber's enlisted Scout Corps. All were malcontents, "bad Indians," who had joined up with Niño during the past weeks of his flight from the consequences of meting out Apache justice to the Indian killer of his father. They were spoiling for a fight with the soldiers, looking for the least excuse to start another Indian war in Arizona. Indeed Niño had promised to lead them into just such a war by coming here tonight. Out in the desert, riding around dodging soldier patrols, it had seemed like something important. The praise from the bad ones had made him feel the size of Cochise, even of Mangas Coloradas. But now the full weight of the decision to "surprise" the soldiers was bearing down upon him.

In his head he still told himself he had done no original wrong, but in his heart he knew better. He had committed a murder and ought now to be on his way to face the white man's justice for his crime. But he had not come here to surrender honestly, as a sergeant of scouts in the United States Army. He had come as an Apache, with quite another thought than peacefully giving himself up to the mercies of the military court. He shook his head for the third time, black eyes brooding unhappily.

"Well?" pressed Lagarto, the Lizard. "What about it? If your insides have turned to water, just say so. It wasn't our father who was killed."

"No," agreed the second Indian, "nor will it be our wickiups which are shamed if you show fear of Seiber."

The third and fourth scouts said nothing. One was a corporal whose stripes had come only through long, hard service, the other, a friend of Niño's. It was Lizard, finally, who broke the stillness.

"What have you decided?" he demanded.

"We will wait till morning," replied Niño flatly. "I won't sneak down there in the dark like an animal. Go back and tell the others to camp where they are."

"Suppose I don't?" challenged the other.

"Lizard," said Niño, "you want to fight me *mano a mano?"*

Lizard blinked rapidly. The *mano a mano* was a hand-to-hand affair with knives and a ruling that one of the contestants be left dead. It was the Apache way of settling academic arguments to the satisfaction of both sides.

"Not tonight," answered the Tonto, after a significant pause, and wheeled his pony to go and halt the others.

The corporal looked at Niño and said, "You have made an enemy." And Niño looked back at him and said, "What is one more? From this night forward, my life will be full of enemies. Come. Let's get down and rest a bit before the sun rises."

The other Indians said nothing. They got down from

their ponies and sat hunched beneath their blankets, smoking and watching the sleeping army camp below.

The next day was June 1, 1887. It was a lovely day, clear and still, the desert sunlight washing everything crystal clean. The Apaches rode into the camp laughing and joking in a loud manner, a very bad sign with Apaches. Al Seiber, big, stolid, warm-natured German-born chief of cavalry scouts, came out of his tent frowning. As he did, Captain Francis Pierce hurried up to join him.

"That's Niño, isn't it?" he asked, and Seiber nodded.

"Yes, he's come in. I thought he would, but I don't care for what he's brought with him. That's a bad bunch."

"Should I put them under arrest? We don't want any trouble."

"Then don't try putting them under arrest," said Seiber shortly. "Let me handle it."

The Apaches were up to the tent, then, a following of San Carlos Indians on foot beginning to gather in their wake. Seiber saluted Niño with a wave and a nod, and the Apache youth returned both. Then the stillness fell.

Seiber, old at these things, let it cook a while; let the Indians grow restless under his calm regard. When he thought they were nervous enough, he nodded again.

"Well, Niño, here we are."

"Yes sir," said the fugitive sergeant.

"I sent for you and you came in."

"Yes, sir."

"Is that all you have to say to me, Niño?"

"No. I have also to say I am sorry for running away. A brave man doesn't run away."

Seiber smiled a little. "It's braver to run away and come back, than to stay in the first place," he said. "I reckon we don't need to debate your courage."

"Thank you. What are you going to do with me?"

They were down to it now. Of a sudden the restless

riders behind Niño grew very still, and Seiber said what he had to say with great care.

"I see you still wear the stripes, Niño."

"Yes sir."

"Then you're still a soldier. Good. Arrest those deserters behind you."

The silence became oppressive. The reservation Indians moved back. A part of the rebel band fell away leaving the knot of eight primary riders bunched with Niño. Seiber committed their faces and names to memory: Say-es, Lac-cohen, Pash-lau-ta, Miguel, Wash-lan-ta-la, Ca-do-day-du-on, Has-tin-tudo-dy and the Tonto, Lagarto. All were his men saving for Lizard, whom he did not know, but would know well from this day.

"Niño," he said, "get their guns."

His companions watched Niño as red desert wolves watch a crippled antelope. He felt their eyes in his back but more than that he felt the eyes of Seiber in his front. He saluted and got off his pony.

"Give me your guns," he said to the others, and began to pass among them collecting the weapons. The last man was Lizard. When Niño reached up for his rifle, he kicked his arm away and fired at Seiber. The bullet struck the big German in the left instep. It caused a wound which remained unhealed to his death, and it started the last Apache war in Arizona.

With the echo of the shot, Seiber was diving for his tent and the Indians, reservation and rebel, were scattering like quail. Niño stampeded with the rest. He ran for his pony. His eight companions retrieved their rifles and spurred out of camp. Niño came on their heels bending low over his mount's neck. Behind them Seiber rushed from his tent, rifle swinging to shoulder. His hurried shot at Lizard missed and hit a bystanding reservation Indian, killing him instantly. At this, the last of the local Apaches disappeared and within seconds of Lizard's treacherous act Camp San Carlos was deserted of red men.

Patrols of cavalry at once went out. The hills nearby were scoured till dark. None of the outlaws was found. When the furor quieted next day, it was learned from the returning reservation Indians that Niño and his followers had ridden south for the Sierra Madre. Their trail, well marked by stolen horses, burned ranch buildings and the murders of three white men, was followed toward the border. One patrol, that of Lieutenant Franklin Johnson, came upon the fugitives as they were going over into Mexico. In a hot skirmish two unknown Indians riding with the wanted group were killed, but Niño and his eight bad ones made the crossing and vanished into the Sonora desert.

For a long while nothing was heard of them, then Niño's name began to be spoken again. More legend than good legal evidence were the embittered testimonies against him and his desperate fellows. One example serves a hundred purposes of refutation. A white whiskey seller was killed on the Rio San Carlos twelve miles above the military camp. Niño was promptly charged with the crime, even though at the moment of its commission he was on the reservation in negotiation with Seiber regarding a surrender. Such the quality of justice for all—Apaches—in Old Arizona.

Once more Niño and his men took up the weary outlaw trail into Sonora. This time they disappeared for months. In the end, however, homesickness and that certain pathetic sense of loyalty to the uniform whose ragged coat he yet wore brought Niño again to Seiber and Camp San Carlos. Contact was successfully made upon this occasion. The repentant youth agreed to come in with all eight of his original followers. First condition of the surrender was that they would be tried by a military court and not turned over to the civil authorities. The Army kept faith. They were tried for desertion by court martial, and convicted. Before sentence was carried out, however, President Cleveland intervened with full pardon for the nine Apaches. Released, the Indians returned to their people upon the reservation. They had hardly come home when the feared civil authorities, determined they must not go free, ordered their arrests on local warrants. They were arraigned and tried in the United States District Court of Judge Joseph H. Kibbey at Globe, Gila County, on the already discredited charge of murdering the San Carlos whiskey seller. Conviction was automatic; evidence was neither required nor produced. On October 18, 1889, Niño and his eight fellows were found guilty and sentenced to seven years each in the Territorial Prison at Yuma.

To nomad Apache horsemen reared upon the lofty cedar-scented mesas of the Mogollon Rim, this was in fact a sentence of death. At Yuma they would be leg-ironed in one five-by-eight feet stone cell. There would be no window and the door would be a strap-steel grating with four-inch openings. The temperatures, driven upward by the tropic air of the Colorado's sea-level delta, would climb to 130° in the shade and cling there, day and night, day after day after day. They would have to fight like panting dogs for the mere breath of life itself. Once inside the prison, they knew they would all be dead within the first twelve months.

For what followed the Army and Sergeant Niño could not be held in account. The one had acted with honor, the other with dignity and courage. Now there was an end to all such decent things. Now there was only Yuma Prison waiting upon its sun-bleached bluff above the Colorado.

It still waits: Niño and his eight men never reached it.

"Glenn," the tall man spoke with urgent softness, "I feel as though it ain't right. Somehow it bothers me."

Sheriff Glenn Reynolds waved aside the dissent.

"Tom," he said, "if I'd rather you took those Indians over the Casa Grande, than to rope agin Charley Meadows in the Phoenix show, I'd surely say so. As it is, I got ten dollars on you and, by God, you're going to Phoenix!"

Tom Horn grinned in his diffident way, and nodded. "Well, all right. It don't seem fitting for a chief deputy to be roping steers at the territorial fair while the sheriff shotguns Apaches over the Pinals. But if that's the way you see it, that's the way she'll be."

"Don't worry about it," shrugged the senior officer. "It ain't like I never took a coachful of Indians over the mountains before."

"No, it ain't," said Horn. "But me knowing their talk, and all, it just worries me to leave you go it alone."

"Alone, hell. I'll have Holmes with me."

"Yeah, I suppose. All the same, I—"

"Out," interrupted Reynolds, pointing to the office door. "You going to stand there all fall arguing how good you are at slinging Apache, Charley'll have the damn contest won and the prize money spent before ever you get your loop shook loose. Now, get!"

"Yes sir," grinned Tom Horn, and got.

An hour later the prisoners left Globe in a big nine-passenger Abbott & Downing coach. Eugene Middleton was driver. Deputy W.H. Holmes was inside sitting guard on the Apaches. The latter were handcuffed, but not leg-ironed. Fifty feet behind the coach, Sheriff Reynolds rode alone, shotgun barred across his saddlehorn ready for any break by the desperate captives. It was a windy morning, turning cold. The date was November 1, 1889. No real trouble was anticipated, none was encountered. They reached Riverside on the Gila sometime after dark that night. They had made forty-two miles from Globe and were feeling better about the whole affair. Some of Tom Horn's uneasiness had worn off on Reynolds and his two companions, but an entire day of watchful waiting had shown them no disposition on the parts of the Apaches to make trouble. In fact, the Indians had not made a sound since leaving Globe, sitting meek and quiet as kittens the entire way. Deputy Holmes allowed that they were finally whipped, and

Reynolds agreed. Driver Middleton's opinion was not solicited.

Next morning the cold had become intense. Reynolds shivered and decided to ride the coach. His horse, lame in the off-shoulder, was left at Riverside to be picked up on the return trip. Reynolds and his deputy both borrowed overcoats and wore them over their guns. They traded off through the morning riding topside with Middleton and inside with the prisoners. There was still no trouble, but now the Apaches were beginning to talk.

At Ripsey Wash, footing the Kelvin grade, the coach struck heavy sand. By the time the horses had dragged it through a quarter mile of this, they were panting and lathered. Starting up the steep pitch of the grade they were already needing the whip. And inside the coach the Indians were talking faster than ever.

Holmes looked at them and ordered them to stop jabbering. But they knew he did not understand their tongue. They only lowered their voices, kept right on talking. The deputy was on the point of calling up to Middleton to stop the stage, when the latter hauled in his teams unbidden. Surprised, Holmes stuck his head out the window.

"What's up?" he asked of Reynolds, who was climbing down stiff with cold.

"Gene says we got to take the Injuns out and walk them up the hill. Says the horses won't pull it otherwise."

The deputy opened his door, stepped into the road.

"Well, that ain't a bad idea. I reckon me and you could use the exercise too. I'm half froze. Besides, them monkeys been doing nothing but talk ever since we left. I figure it's time we broke up the meeting for a spell. Fact is, I was just going to yell up to you to pull in."

"Injun talk don't mean nothing, Holmes. You'd ought to know that by this time."

"Yeah, mebbe. All the same, I wish we had old Tom along. He savvies that baboon chatter of theirs like no white man ought. He could tell us quick enough what they're saying."

"I done told you. They ain't saying nothing."

"Yeah, I heard you. I'd still rather hear it from Tom Horn."

Reynolds scowled at him. It was a bad day for dispositions. Or for arguing with deputies.

"Get them out," he ordered abruptly. "Next election you can vote for Tom Horn for sheriff. Meanwhile, I'm still wearing the star."

"You bet," said Holmes, and herded the Apaches out.

Reynolds let five of the eight Indians—one of Niño's companions had been held in Globe on a separate murder charge—climb out of the coach, then said quickly:

"That's enough. I want Niño, Pash-lau-ta and Say-es left inside. That's to guarantee good conduct from their little friends with us."

"How about Avota?" asked Holmes.

Jesus Avota, a Mexican horse thief, was incidental baggage to the Yuma assignment of Apache outlaws. He was in no way dangerous and Reynolds rather liked him.

"Jesus," he called, "you want to stretch a leg, pile on out here. Hurry it up, we ain't got all day."

The Mexican stumbled out. Middleton shook up his horses, started the lightened stage uphill. Reynolds waved Avota to go ahead of him. The Mexican led off. Behind him came Reynolds, then the five Apaches, then Holmes in the rear. The party kept about one hundred feet back of the slow-moving coach. The Indians, now, were very quiet, saying nothing. Ahead, the road hairpinned sharply. A boulder the size of a small cabin stood in the crook of the switchback. As the stage disappeared behind this landmark, Miguel, first behind Reynolds, lifted his manacled hands and dropped their taut chain over the sheriff's head, pinning his arms and holding him virtually helpless. In the same instant, the remaining four Apaches jumped Holmes.

The latter, subject to heart spells, fainted. As he slumped, Lizard, the Tonto, seized his rifle and shot him through the chest. Leaving Holmes to his companions, the Tonto leaped at the struggling Reynolds, who, handicapped by his overcoat, was only now clearing his revolver. The weapon, however, came out too late. As Reynolds raised it to blow out the ribs of Miguel, Lizard put the muzzle of Holmes' rifle to the back of the sheriff's neck and pulled the trigger. Reynolds died before Miguel could free himself of his body, his spine shattered, his head nearly severed by the point-blank blast of the heavy charge.

Jesus Avota, paralyzed witness to the murders, now ran belatedly up the stageroad, trying to get around the landmark rock before his turn should come. Lizard raised the rifle to cut him down, but Miguel stopped him.

"No," he ordered, "let him go. What can he do to us?"

"Bah!" growled Lizard. "You and your damned Mexican grandmother!" It was true that Miguel was but three-quarters Apache. The brown blood made him weak and he admitted it to his friends. But this Tonto was no friend.

He picked up Sheriff Reynolds's six-gun.

"You want to shoot somebody, shoot me," he said.

Lizard might have done it but the others came up just then. "Come on," yelled one of them. "I think Niño is in trouble. I don't hear any noise up there." Another said, "That's right; let's go," and they all ran for the boulder and the bend in the stageroad.

As they did, Avota was just coming up with the coach. Middleton, who had heard the shots from Holmes' rifle, hauled up his teams, climbed inside the coach and covered Niño and his two companions with his Colt. Niño at once called out, "I'll sit here, don't shoot!" and Middleton answered, "Yes, that's right, you will. For if a one of you moves, I will drill you, center, Niño. This is your doings."

"No," said Niño, "not mine."

But as Avota panted up and Middleton for one instant took his eyes from his prisoners, Pash-lau-ta leaped past him, into the road, and away back toward the boulder. In the same moment Miguel rounded the boulder. He had picked up Sheriff Reynolds' Winchester carbine, and he now tossed the weapon to Pash-lau-ta, as Middleton leaned from the coach window to draw a bead on the fugitive. Pash-lau-ta caught the carbine, whirled and fired from the hip. The shot struck Middleton in the adam's apple, a glancing hit which toppled the driver out the stagedoor and sprawling into the road, where he lay motionless.

Niño and Say-es now leaped out of the coach. Miguel had the sheriff's keys. Niño took them and set the others free. While his back was turned with this work, Pash-lau-ta put the rifle-muzzle to Middleton's head. Miguel warned Niño, who turned on Pash-lau-ta with a barking order for him to save the round of ammunition.

"He is dead," he told his savage fellow, "and we need every bullet."

"All right," snapped Pash-lau-ta, raising the steel-shod butt of the weapon, "I'll just cave his head in with this."

"Woman's work!" sneered Niño. "If you want to cave in some heads, go back and make sure of the sheriff and his deputy. They're the ones whose law has made us murderers."

"That's right," admitted Pash-lau-ta. "I hadn't thought of it. Come on," he said to the others. "Who wants to help me spread out their brains?"

Four went with him, Say-es and Miguel staying with Niño. Jesus Avota stood to one side, afraid to speak, afraid, even, to breathe. When his comrades had gone Miguel looked at Niño and nodded to the body of Middleton, starting to say something. Niño warned him with a glance, and a movement of his head toward Say-es.

"Say-es," he said, "take the Mexican and cut loose the horses. Then let the Mexican go free. As for us, we must mount up and get away from here."

This was the simple truth and the other Apache went swiftly to do as bid.

"Niño!" burst out Miguel, when Say-es had gone, "that white man lying there is alive! He is pretending to be dead. Are you thinking to leave him here?"

"Why not? You know he's alive, I know he's alive; the others don't. Isn't that a good thing? Aren't you glad about it?"

"What do you mean, Niño?"

"We're different than the others, that's what. I'm a sergeant, you're a corporal. We're soldiers, not savages."

Miguel shook his head. "The others would have killed him," he frowned. "Does that mean you are saying they are savages?"

"No, only that you and I are not."

"But why? You and I were in the plan the same as they were. We all talked of it. We all knew it would happen. Where's the difference, then, between them and ourselves?"

Niño looked at him steadily. "Don't you know where it is, Miguel?" he said.

The other Apache returned his look, then dropped his fierce gaze. "Yes," he answered, pointing to the chevrons on his tattered shirtsleeve, "it's right here."

2

The pursuit was vigorous, if a day delayed.

Middleton, half dead, crawled back to Riverside. His journey would have made an epic of frontier lore in itself had it not been overlain by the larger event. It was not until dawn of the following day, however, nearly twenty-four hours later, that a barking dog found his bloody form in the ditch beyond the town culvert. A big posse swarmed out of Riverside within the hour. The news of the Kelvin Grade Massacre was put on the telegraph. Cavalry detachments from Forts Grant, Apache, Huachuca, McDowell and Lowell were in the field by nightfall. The following day, and the next, there was no break in the blank silence of juniper and greasewood which hid the red fugitives. Then a posse from Globe struck their trail, running it hotly to the mouth of the San Pedro River. Here darkness halted the chase. Reinforcements, including a troop of Third Cavalry, were rushed to the spot. Before dawn a hundred men were gathered in readiness to stay on the track until the last of the escaped murderers was run to earth. Sunrise blighted their grim purpose. The wily renegades were not to be so simply taken. Two miles from the campsite, the Apache ponies fanned out on eight separate courses. The land ahead was rising sharply, going over to rock and granite wastes where sight-tracking of single trails was hopeless. The white curses were loud and ugly, but futile as wind blowing sandgrains against a mountain. Packrat, who came with

Seiber and the Third Cavalry as the best of the remaining Indian scouts, said it most succinctly.

"What's the use?" he shrugged. "It's Niño."

"Yep," said Seiber, equally brief. "Let's go home."

Now the first dark month fled. Each week produced some new report of atrocities by Niño and his "killer pack." Useful evidence, as usual, was lacking. By the common law of the land, as conducted in the older settlements, no single case could have been kept in court a day. All would have been thrown out after preliminary hearing. But in Old Arizona all parties, red and white, were eager to blame the "damned 'Pache" for any crime of their own, or their neighbor's. It was so much easier simply to lay the murder or the rape or the ranch-burning to "that devil Niño" than to seek out the real criminal. Repeatedly, the Apache youth was able to offer—usually by sending word in to Seiber—proof of his presence miles from the scene of the particular offense. In turn, Seiber did his best to contact Niño and induce him to surrender peacefully. All the while, however, that he was attempting to call in his man for conference, he was seeking as well to take him afield. This was consistent with Army policy which held the working rule for Indians to be, "if they can't be seduced, shoot them." Niño accepted this policy and did not regard Seiber as his enemy. They were soldiers fighting a war. Had their situations been reversed, he would have hunted the white man as relentlessly. And the option to the hunt was not unfair: if Niño would surrender, he would be given fair treatment; if he would not surrender, Seiber would run him to earth like an animal. Apache law would operate the same, with a technical exception—Apache law contained no provision for surrender.

Through November the Army kept troops in pressing pursuit of the eight Yuma consignees. In December the number of patrols was suddenly reduced. But the Army had not called off the chase, only changed the hounds. Niño was receiving advance information on every detachment sent out to apprehend him and his followers; counter-espionage was indicated and implemented. Seiber sent for Packrat.

The plump Apache with the trailing eye next only to Niño's had earned his name as a thief of things minor about the post. But he was not without some shred of that honor supposed to prevail among the light-fingered. When informed of what Seiber had in view, he at once drew himself to his full five feet and one inch.

"There are many things a man will do for money," he said, "and some few he will not. Of that few is the matter of betraying a friend."

"Nonsense!" exclaimed Seiber. "It's for his own good that we want to catch him. You know that."

"Yes, and I also know that you will never catch him. Not without killing him. And you know that."

"Bah! You're a damned rascal! You would sell your grandmother's heart for a day's pay!"

"Sure I would. But my grandmother is dead, and my friend is still alive."

"You sneaking dog, I'll take you off the company rolls!"

"Do it and I will join Niño."

"Hah! I'll throw you in the guardhouse first!"

"Do that also. Then you won't get one Apache scout to go any place for you."

"I'll remember this, you fat rogue!"

"Of course. How could you forget asking a man to betray his friend?"

Seiber grimaced helplessly. "Go," he said, "and stay out of my sight a long time. You're a disgrace to us all."

Packrat nodded philosophically. "You want me to find Nosey for you while I'm hiding in shame?" he asked.

Seiber had to grin, wondering how these simple-minded Indians were so continually able to read his thoughts.

"Yes," he said, "and Josh, too."

"Well, naturally," shrugged Packrat, turning. "Can the buzzard circle without his shadow following him?"

"Go to hell," growled Seiber, "but be quick about it."

Packrat went the last mile up the mesa trail very careful to sing his Apache prayer song good and loud. With two nervous ones like Josh and Eskinospas it never paid to take chances. Especially when those two were deserters and under a murder charge. Presently a rifle bullet whined off a rock in front of his mustang's nose and Packrat held up in the trail and called out, "It's only me, Packrat, you damn fools! Can't you see yet? Are you still blind with *tizwin*?" There was a little stretch of silence, then some laughing from above, and Josh called back, "No, hell, we're all out of *tizwin*. Did you bring any? Come on up."

Packrat started his pony again. Topping the rocky incline, he came into the little niche on the mesa's wall where the guilty ones were camped. Reaching his Army canteen from the saddlehorn, he tossed it to Eskinospas.

"Here, Nosey, a gift from Seiber," he said. "Good hospital whiskey. A whole quart."

Nosey caught the canteen, uncorked it suspiciously, sniffed, gasped, broke into a beatific smile.

"By Yosen's navel!" he cried, "it *is* whiskey!"

"Never mind Yosen's navel," said Packrat. "It's not Apache gods you are needing right now. Am I right?"

Neither Josh nor Nosey were unusually keen of mind. They were only the number three and four trailers of Seiber's San Carlos Indian police force. It was their skill and not good sense for which they were presently being wooed back to duty. Not understanding this just yet, they scowled and stepped back.

"What is that?" said Nosey, picking up his rifle.

"Nothing," said Packrat quickly. "Just that Seiber says there's another canteen of this good whiskey for you if you want to be smart."

"No!" muttered Josh, frowning. "The last time we were smart and listened to Seiber he sent us up to that secret *tizwin* party at Fort Apache. We were supposed to be smart, then, and to get him some information from those damned Salt Rivers about Niño. You remember? Yes, sure you do. And what happened? Those devils got us drunk and into a fight and we killed one of them and here we are sitting up in this stinking eagle's nest with no food and no water and no news of Niño and you sneaking up here and trying to bribe us with whiskey and get us drunk again so that Seiber can come in behind you and take us for that murder. Oh, no, fat one! you don't fool us as easily as all that." He, too, now reached for his gun and Packrat put up both hands in a hurry.

"Look!" he said, "I don't even have a pistol with me. I came here to offer you a chance to get out of bad trouble. Would I turn on my own friends? Now you better listen, for you know what will happen to you if Seiber gets mad and comes after you. You'll go to Florida with Geronimo and the others. You think you'd like that?"

It was a sobering thought. The two fugitive scouts put down their rifles. They even put down the canteen of whiskey.

"No," said Josh. "What is the deal?"

"Very simple," answered Packrat. "You two are going to find out where Niño and his band are. They know that you are running from that murder at Fort Apache. They will let you join them. You can win their trust and stay with them and learn all their plans and hiding places and when the time is right you can let Seiber know and he will come in and clean them up. If you do that, Seiber says you will go free, that you can have your jobs back."

He hesitated, watching them. They went off a little ways and talked it over. It wasn't easy. Packrat picked up the canteen and went over to them. "Here," he said, "this will help you think." They took the whiskey and drank some of it. Then they drank some more. Pretty soon the canteen rang empty when they put it on the rock nearby. They knocked it off, laughingly listened to it bounce and bang down the cliffside, went back over to Packrat and said thickly, "All right. Tell Seiber we will do it."

Packrat nodded and got back on his pony.

"There is only one other little thing," he told them. "Seiber wants some evidence that you have truly found Niño's band. He isn't going to come chasing any more wild fox tracks, you understand? He wants *something* this time. See that you bring it to him."

Josh and Nosey nodded in return.

"We will bring him something," said Nosey. And Josh said, "Yes, you tell Seiber that. You tell him we will bring it right to his tent."

"I'll tell him," said Packrat, and wheeled his pony.

Two weeks and a day later the enlisted Apache scouts Josh and Eskinospas rode into Camp San Carlos, a bloody Indian blanket slung from the horn of the latter's saddle. They stopped in front of Seiber's tent. The Chief of Scouts opened the flap and peered out, then asked them to dismount and come in. They did so, Nosey bringing the carelessly rolled blanket.

Inside, neither Apache said anything. Nosey unfurled the blanket, spilling a battered human head out upon the dirt floor at Seiber's feet. Seiber stared down at it, and only nodded quietly.

"All right, that's Pash-lau-ta. How about the others?"

"All dead," said Josh, "except Say-es. He, we wounded bad, but he got away to the river."

Seiber eyed them narrowly.

"*All* dead?" he asked slowly. "*Only* Say-es escaped?"

The two Apaches shifted their moccasined feet.

"Well," said Nosey, "almost all."

"Then Niño got away, too, is that it?" Seiber demanded.

"No," said Josh, "not quite it."

"Then, what?" said the white man harshly.

Nosey shrugged. "He wasn't even there. We never saw Niño. We found the band in four days. They were up on Saddle Mountain. Then we waited nine days for Niño to appear. He never did. We got nervous and shot the others in their blankets. Except Say-es, as we said."

"That's the truth," added Josh. "When do we get our jobs back? And where's that other whiskey?"

"Wait a minute," said Seiber, "I ain't through with Niño yet. How come he wasn't with Pash-lau-ta and the others?"

"Pash-lau-ta said that a little while after they killed the sheriff and his deputy and all the soldier patrols were riding after them night and day, Niño said it wasn't fair that he stay with them. He said the soldiers were after him and that if he stayed with the others it would only bring sorrow on them. So he went off alone one night and they didn't see him after that."

"Is that all?"

"Well, almost. Lizard didn't trust Niño, and he went off after him the next day."

"Damn!" exploded Seiber frustratedly. "First you say you got them all. Then Say-es gets away, wounded. Then Niño is gone before you get there. Then that blasted Tonto shags off after Niño, also before you get there. Now how many *did* you get? And, remember, you will have to lead me to their bodies up there."

Nosey and Josh consulted in Apache, counting and recounting on their fingers. Finally they nodded in agreement, and Nosey turned back to Seiber.

"Five," he said. "There were eight that you sent us after. Niño, Lizard and Say-es got away. That's five left up there. Yes, you will find five bodies on Saddle Mountain. Just follow the buzzards."

"That's right," said a voice behind them. "Just what I have been doing."

The two Apaches whirled to see Packrat, dusty and sweat-stained, standing by the tent flaps.

"You!" cried Josh. "What have you been up to?"

"What I said, following the buzzards."

"He means you two," said Seiber. Then, quickly to Packrat. "You say they are telling the truth?"

"Yes, there's five dead Indians up there on Saddle Mountain. All shot in the head. That is, after the head was crushed with the rock."

"But no Niño?"

"No Niño."

"How about Say-es?"

"He won't go far. I trailed him into the rocks by the river. He can't walk and I took his pony. He'll be there when we go for him; we will get him."

"We will," agreed Seiber. "And he'll get life in Yuma."

"Death, you mean," said Packrat, and Seiber nodded, knowing the wild Say-es would die like a mountain stallion in the stinking cells of the territorial prison.

"How about the Tonto?" he asked grimly.

"Lizard? I could get no lasting track on him. He's pretty clever, you know. For a Tonto, that is."

"You got no idea where he went?"

"I didn't say that. I know very well where he went. He went after Niño. And I can tell you more; he will stay after him. It's the girl."

"The girl—?" said Seiber softly.

"Yes, surely you know the one?"

"No," said the big German, "no, I don't. Tell me about her. Tell me *all* about her. I didn't know Niño was one for the women."

"He isn't. Only for this one."

"And Lizard's got his eye on her, too, eh?"

"Yes. Like she was a fly on a rock."

Seiber nodded thoughtfully. "Thank you," he said. "Thank you very much."

3

The girl's name was Chuana. She was the daughter of Eskim-in-zim, co-chief of the Aravaipa Apache, named by him for his fellow chief, Chil-chu-ana. To Seiber, when he learned her identity, it seemed a simple matter of plucking up the slender desert flower and replanting her closer to San Carlos headquarters, where her cultivation could be more carefully controlled. But the Army never did the simple thing. When apprised by Seiber that Niño was being lip-fed news of troop movements, as well as warm kisses, by his dark-eyed sweetheart, the agent, John Bullis, ordered San Carlos commandant Captain Lewis Johnson to seize as prisoners of war all seventy-five of the combined peoples of Eskim-in-zim and Chil-chu-ana. Subsequently, Bullis directed the removal of the friendly Aravaipa to far-off Fort Union, New Mexico. Here, the children were separated from their parents and shipped out to the Ramona Indian School in Santa Fe. It was a cruel and stupid judgment rendered in place of Seiber's sane and logical and kind recommendation to restrain Chuana only, and it cost the Chief of Scouts his job, a part of his reputation, his rightful place in Arizona history and his last chance to bring in Niño peaceably.

The order, actually, was not carried out until March of 1890, but when Bullis suggested it in face of Seiber's December 1889 proposal to merely chaperon the Apache girl, the stolid German lost his temper.

"By God, Bullis," he said, "you do that and I quit."

Bullis was a captain by rank, and was so called by

all at San Carlos. Seiber, twenty years and more in the regular army, could scarcely have left out the title by accident. The agent's face grew dark with fury. He didn't like Al Seiber, and never had. The big German loved the Apache, there could be little doubt. As certainly, he detested Agent John Bullis. He stood six feet and two inches tall, weighed two hundred and twenty-two pounds, of which perhaps two pounds was something softer than bone and muscle and tough Teutonic determination. Bullis was afraid of him, and his voice shook with emotion as he now answered his deep-growled warning.

"*Captain* Bullis," he seethed, face livid.

"The devil!" rumbled Seiber. "You're not fit to command a platoon, and I'll not serve where you're stationed another day. I'm asking Captain Johnson for a transfer when I leave these quarters."

Bullis controlled himself. "That won't be necessary," he rasped. "Your term of service is up as of now, Seiber. When you walk out that door, you're on your way to look for new work."

"That," said Al Seiber, saluting him with deliberate overflourish, "is the most intelligent thing you've said since you enlisted. Good-day to you, *Captain* Bullis, and bad luck."

Fortunately or unfortunately, the incident was unwitnessed. Hence, when Captain Johnson heard of it and went to persuade both Bullis and Seiber to forget it, he was able to effect a working truce between the two. But where the camp didn't know of the clash, its two principals had stated their respective cases with entire accuracy as to all save precise dates. The end was not long, nor did it alter the terms. On November 1, the following year, Al Seiber and the Army came to their final parting. Nothing was said, then or later, as to the details of the dismissal, either by the old scout or by the government he had served so long and in a position which has been conservatively called "probably the most dangerous ever filled by a white man in the Southwest."

In the eleven months of Seiber's grace, December 1889—November 1890, little was heard of Niño. The Apache people, alienated anew by the brutal treatment afforded Eskim-in-zim and Chil-chu-ana, reacted by furnishing the outlaw of the San Carlos with more aid and comfort than at any previous time. Concurrently, they quit talking to Seiber and in his last efforts to contact Niño he was virtually helpless. The failures were not his fault, but that of the impossible handicap Bullis had imposed upon him by the Aravaipa removal order. Nonetheless, they reflected seriously on his former stature, and when he left the government service in November he did so as a discredited legend. It was typical of big, quiet, good-natured Al Seiber that, when informed at last and icily by Bullis of his dismissal, he only nodded and said, "Thank you, Captain. Now I can get on with my work."

Bullis, of course, misunderstood him.

"You don't seem to understand, Seiber," he said. "This time Johnson won't save you. You're through. Finished. Done."

Seiber shrugged, pushed back his weather-stained hat.

"Well, Captain," he said, "you see it your way, I see it mine. Way I see it, I set out to do a job here and I ain't quite finished with it."

Bullis nodded condescendingly. "Perhaps we might find something for you," he said. "We could use a corral man for the packmules, I suppose."

Seiber grinned. It was a little twisted and a little sad but it was a grin. "Not quite what I had in mind, Captain," he said. "I didn't set out to clean up any mule corrals but I did set out to clean up another matter and I reckon I will do it with or without the Army."

"Look here, Seiber," said Bullis sharply, thinking the words held a threat for him, "if you try making any more trouble around here . . ."

Seiber shook his head, pulled his old hat forward, interrupted quietly. "Don't hardly think it will be around here," he said. "Leastways, not lately it ain't been."

"What the devil are you talking about?" demanded the confused Bullis.

"Niño," answered Al Seiber, and turned and went out of the agent's office and out of the service of the Third U.S. Cavalry at San Carlos. The only epitaph the Army ever wrote for him was a three-word entry in the regimental record, under the heading; *Seiber, A.*; *Scout*:

"Dropped," it said, "cause unknown."

4

Niño stared off into the night. It was lonely in the Pedregosas. They were dry mountains lying but an hour's pony ride from the Mexican border. Nothing lived in them but the thorny and horned things of the desert. No one came there. If they did, a man could see them from far off, and be ready for them. The Pedregosas were Indian mountains and always had been. They were safe and certain shelter from the white man but, oh! they were a lonesome and homesick place.

Homesick? thought Niño. No, he wasn't homesick. He was heartsick. He wanted to see Chuana. He wanted to see her more than he had ever wanted anything in his life. Even more than he had wanted to prove to Seiber that he hadn't done all those evil things charged to him. But Agent Bullis had sent Chuana to the Indian school in New Mexico. And he had discharged Seiber from the Army. So Niño stayed in the Pedregosas and wondered where his white friend had gone, and what the people at the Indian school were doing to Chuana, his *nah-lin*, his young Aravaipa sweetheart. But the lonely winds and the long, hungry months had brought no news of Chuana and no news of Seiber.

Niño had wandered the Sierra Madres of Mexico trying to find a new life. He had visited the secret camp of his people down there—the seven Chiricahuas who had escaped from Geronimo's surrender in Skeleton Canyon, and the one warrior, Massai, who had gotten away from the train guards in Missouri and come home almost a thousand miles on foot and alone. But, though they welcomed him and bade him stay with them, he could not bring his heart to forget Chuana, nor his honor to forget Seiber. And so he had come, after a long time, back up to sit in the Pedregosas and pine away for his *nah-lin* and his *schichobe*, his great and good friend, Seiber.

Now a year, and more, had gone. It was the first month of the new year, 1891. Niño was cold and lonely and ill-fed and surely the soldiers had quit looking for him so hard by this time. Why should he not go home a little now? Why would they want to hurt him any longer? Why not just get on that old ribby horse he had hidden in the rocks behind him and ride out of this friendless place and go home to see his people at San Carlos?

With the wishful, longing thought, Niño stirred himself. He stood up, drawing his worn blanket about his shoulders. It was only a little over a hundred miles. In three nights on his old horse he could be there. If he were lucky and found a new horse, two nights. He looked again northward, then nodded, saying something in Apache.

Going for the old horse, he already knew how he would ride it to avoid trouble. He would follow the Pedregosa trail up into the Chiricahua Mountains and through them, easterly, to strike San Simon Creek. He would go down that stream, north by west, to the stage-line crossing where old Mangas Coloradas used to hold up the Overland Mail Company coaches for a ransom of one wagon of shelled corn to pass safely through on the Tucson run from Lordsburg and El Paso. Then he would follow the creek and the military supply route to the Gila River and down that stream to the reservation and the *rancherias* of his people.

When he swung up on the winter-ragged mustang, the aging brute seemed to sense that they were homeward-bound. He went down out of the arid rocks of the Pedregosas and stepping along the secret Indian road over the Chiricahuas to San Simon crossing as though he were four years old and a proud-cut stud, rather than a packhorse gelding which would never see his sixteenth summer again. So well did he go, in fact, and so well went Niño's plan to avoid detection by boldly riding the army's wagonroad route from the crossing up to San Carlos, that he brought his Apache master to the scarps of Chutanay Mesa overlooking the *rancheria* of Na-chay-go-tah, the Packrat, just with the ending of the second night. Niño did not wait for the sunrise, but went down to the *rancheria* quickly and furtively, before the long purple shadows of the retreating dark should pull back to the mesa's foot, letting the sudden flood of pink and aquamarine daylight illumine each least pebble and prickly pear unsheltered on the barren floor of the Gila's wide valley.

His friend was at home and glad to see him. After the first exchange of Apache blessings and white man's firm handshakes, Niño did not use his host's tribal name again, but got at once down to the business which had brought him here, and to the good-sounding, direct use of old-time names.

"Packrat," he said, "I am sick and have come home to get well. Will you help me?"

The pudgy brave elevated his shoulders. "A minute ago we called each other *schicho* and *schichobe*," he said. "Does a man say 'friend' and 'great friend,' only to turn away and cover his ears?"

"No, of course not. You will forgive me, old friend. I have been alone too long and I am sick."

"You have said that twice now. Where are you sick?"

"Here," said Niño, pointing to his heart.

"I thought as much. It's that Aravaipa girl."

"Yes, Chuana."

Following the charge and the admission there was a little awkward silence. It was plain that Packrat did not approve of young girls for old friends. But, as he had said, neither did he use the word 'friend' in idleness. His frown deepened.

"I suppose you're going to ask me if I know how to find her for you," he said gruffly. "Well, save yourself the trouble. Of course I can find her. Was I not with the Indian police who guarded the Aravaipa when that fool Bullis had them sent to Fort Union?"

"It was that knowledge which brought me back to see you," said Niño honestly. "I thought about it for a whole year. Then I couldn't resist it. You're the only one who can help me."

"There's another," said Packrat. "If you have the courage to go see him."

Niño's dark eyes flashed. "You mean Seiber?" he cried. "You know where he is? You have found him? He is well. . . ?"

"Wait, wait, only ten things at a time," scowled the other. "Naturally, I know where he is. Was he not my great friend too?"

"Of course. And he is well?"

"He's all right. He finds trouble getting work."

"That's because the agent dismissed him."

"Yes. Others think something was wrong."

"The agent knew that would happen."

"Yes, he did it on purpose that way. He was afraid of Seiber. And jealous of him."

"He was wrong. Seiber was our friend; the best the Apache ever will have."

"Sure." Packrat shrugged again. "But when you're a

good friend of the Apache, you're a bad friend of the white man. It isn't all Bullis's fault that Seiber has trouble finding work."

"You mean we are to blame too?"

"Some of us."

"Like me?"

"Yes, you, Niño. Seiber gave you many chances. You always shied off at the last minute."

"I know, I know. . . ."

Packrat reached over, put a chubby hand on his friend's lean shoulder. "Well, don't look so sad about it," he said. "You can't help it if you are of the *cimmarones*; you can't help it if you're of the outlaw blood. Some of us are and some of us are not. You're wild, I'm not wild. That's the way Yosen planned it."

"He planned it a bad way, then," said Niño. "If a man is wild in his heart and not wild in his mind, he can't do what is right. Everything he does hurts either his Indian friend or his white friend."

Packrat nodded, "It's true," he said, "you've had a bad time of it. Not all your fault either. But maybe we can make it different for you now. Maybe if we find that girl for you and if you have another long talk with Seiber something can now be done. It's been a year and more that you've been hiding down in the Mother Mountains, and I haven't heard a white killing or an Indian rape blamed on you since last spring. I really think the thing to do is go to Seiber and see what he says."

"All right, I'd like that."

"We'll go tonight. He's only over in the Pinals looking for gold. We'll be with him before it gets light tomorrow. He'll tell us what to do. All right?"

Niño's dark head bobbed in agreement. The first smile in many months lit his drawn face fleetingly.

"*Anh*, yes," he said softly in Apache.

Wallapai Clark came to an elbow, listening intently.

The stillness inside the tiny cabin on upper Fish Creek grew so loud he could hear his own heart beating.

"Scanlon!" he whispered, "you awake?"

"Yeah." The voice of his partner came from the opposite bunk. "What you think?"

"It's five A.M. Seiber ain't due back till noon."

Scanlon, not so old to the country as the other man, gulped noisily. "Well, could be a lion after the horses," he suggested hopefully.

"Ummm," said Wallapai, shaking his head. "Lion don't wait to so late. He make a kill now he wouldn't have time to tote it up the hill 'fore daylight."

"Maybe it *is* Seiber, then." Scanlon's feet thumped on the board floor. "I'll holler out the winder and . . ."

"Get away from that winder!" rasped Wallapai Clark. "You make so much as a floorboard squeak, I'll drill you!" He was out of his own bunk, reaching for his Winchester. Moving to the lighter square of gray which indicated the paneless opening in the north wall, he peered out. To Scanlon the seconds seemed twenty-four hours long.

"See anything?" he whispered hoarsely.

"Yeah—nothing."

"What you mean, 'yeah, nothing'? This ain't any time for jokes. That might be Injuns out there."

"That's what I said. When you don't see nothing, that's when 'Paches are about. Shut up."

Scanlon held his breath.

"Two of them," said Wallapai. "Out back of the stock corral."

"How you know, two?"

"Watching the horses' ears. I can make them out in silhouette. Getting a little gray out now. Your bay's flicking his one way, my brown's flagging his the other. That means they got wind of two separate bucks—or maybe bunches."

"My God, Ed! They ain't been any 'Paches around since Niño disappeared in December of Ninety!"

"That's what I know. It's him I'm thinking of."

The silence settled in. Edward A. "Wallapai" Clark had gotten his nickname from his service as chief of Wallapai Indian scouts for the Army in the Geronimo campaign of Eighty-six. More to the moment's importance, he had taken an oath to get Niño back in Eighty-nine, when the latter was publicly blamed for the murder of Clark's then-partner, Bill Diehl. He had sent word via the Apaches to the outlaw of his intention. Niño had replied to the message with his usual protest of innocence, and offer to furnish proof if granted the safe opportunity to do so. Clark had not been interested in the word of an Indian, and had said so. His vow had been largely forgotten in the following long absence of Niño in Mexico, but Scanlon was remembering it now.

"You still think he'd come back and try to get you, Ed?" he asked. "It don't seem to make sense."

"Not to a white man, maybe."

"But, damn it . . ."

"But damn it nothing!" snapped Wallapai. "What the hell you think brought Al Seiber to throw in with us on this here Fish Creek claim? He's in for only ten percent against your fifty and my forty. That don't hardly pay him bean money!"

"Well, I thought maybe it was account of him being sort of down on his luck since getting the can tied to him at San Carlos. You said at the time you let him in that it was only for his being an old soldier comrade."

"Sure, that was a part of it. He got a raw deal and I could well afford to give him ten percent off my half. But you can bet your winter's clean-up that he didn't throw in with us for no measly one-tenth partnership on this claim. He knows gold. And that ain't what he was after."

Scanlon was not too quick. He thought hard, while the minutes crawled by and Wallapai kept his eye, and the muzzle of the Winchester, prowling the horse corral. Finally he muttered uneasily.

"You mean Seiber's after Niño too?"

"Sure. He figured all the time that I'd draw him in." He said it a little bitterly, and Scanlon frowned, puzzled.

"I thought he was supposed to be friends with the damn Injun. I don't get it."

Outside, a cactus owl hooted softly from the direction of the piñon behind the corral. Wallapai put his cupped hands to his lips and answered the call. His imitation was so startlingly real that Scanlon twitched and growled out an angry curse.

"Damn it to hell!" he said, "warn a man when you're gonna hoot in his ear, will you!"

His answer was the palm of Wallapai's hand slapped over his mouth, and a replying curse. "Keep your damn mouth shut! You'll scare 'em off!"

"Well, Jesus," complained the other miner, "ain't that what we want?"

"Not hardly," whispered Wallapai. "If I can call 'em into the open, I can put 'em down. I got shooting light now. Hold still and hush up; here goes another hoot. . . ."

He gave the owl call again, but there was no reply to it and the stillness grew deeper as the winter-morning gray crept down the mountainside. Clark waited with the patience of a stalking cat. His companion, however, grew restless.

"It still bothers me about Al Seiber," he said. "For long as I been in this country, I ain't heard nothing but what a good friend of the 'Pache he is. Now you tell me he's as hot to get this Niño as you are. It don't figure."

For the first time, Clark broke his eyes momentarily from their pre-dawn vigil over the murky corral fencing.

"There's more than one way of wanting to get a man," he said acidly, "or of getting a wanted man. You pan that gravel, Scanlon?"

"You mean . . ." began the other, but Clark cut him off.

"Yeah," he said. "Seiber wants him alive."

Before Scanlon could more than nod slowly to this, Clark cursed and fired three shots at the north end of the corral. In the second that he had removed his eyes from the mountainside, a crouched figure had scuttled forward toward the cover of the woodpile behind the cabin. Now, as Scanlon watched, a second figure rose up from the brush south of the stock-pen and began firing at the window. Clark hit the floor, taking his slower companion with him. When the rifle-burst had subsided and he again risked a glance over the bullet-chewed sill, he was in time to wing three more shots after the vanishing smudges of two mounted Indians driving hard around the up-canyon turn of the Fish Creek Trail.

"Did you get 'em?" asked Scanlon from the floor.

Wallapai Clark shook his head.

"No," he said, "but I *saw* him."

"Him?" said Scanlon.

"Niño," said Clark. "I would know him in the blind-dark of a bat cave. It was him."

Scanlon got up awkwardly from the floor. He looked out the window, into the thinning night. Something about the deliberate calling-in and shooting of unknown men—even Indians—disturbed his plodding mind.

"I dunno, Ed," he said, frowningly. "That still ain't much light to be calling face and features in. Maybe they was friendly."

"And maybe you're going to start telling me how to identify 'Paches!" snapped the other. "But I doubt it like hell. That was Niño, yonder. I seen his soldier coat and sergeant's stripes. But I didn't need them. I'd know that red murderer naked as the day he come into the world. It was him, I tell you, come to kill me."

Again the stubborn Scanlon shook his head.

"I still don't know, Ed," he worried. "Fact it was him and fact he come here, don't have to mean he come here to kill you."

"What the hell do you mean?" demanded Clark scathingly. "Can't you get nothing through that thick Irish skull of yours? If he didn't come to kill me, just what in hell you reckon brung him here? Sweet Christian charity?"

"Well," said Scanlon, honest blue eyes asquint with the continued effort to concentrate, "it's no more than a hunch, Ed, and I suppose you ain't going to take to it kindly, seeing's how you feel, but mebbe—just mebbe, now—that pore damn Injun only come here to see Al Seiber."

Wallapai Clark shot him a look that would have withered a piñon-root. "Hunches like that," he said, "will wind you up where that bone head of yours won't do you much good, and that's under a 'Pache crushing rock, you hear?"

"Sure, sure, Ed, I was only thinking . . ."

"Bad habit," growled Wallapai, "in 'Pache country; especially for white men with hard heads and soft hearts. Get the flapjacks going while I check the horses."

"Sure, Ed, whatever you say," answered Scanlon. But he was still at the window, still staring out into the gray January daylight long after the other man had gone out with the Winchester to see that their precious saddlemounts had not been tampered with, and to cut for moccasin prints or other Indian sign which might establish the identity of the two redmen and so justify his cold-blooded luring-in and attempted killing of them.

Clark always said it was Niño that he saw that morning; that he'd had a clear and certain view of the legendary chevrons and ragged cavalry coat. John Scanlon, who had had the same view, never said anything. He knew his eyes were not as good as those of Wallapai Clark. He also knew when to close his mouth and keep his hunches to himself. He was, after all, only an ignorant hardrock miner, not a famous Indian scout.

5

A straight line drawn upon a map from the Fish Creek country to the old Indian town of Gallup, in New Mexico, stretches some 200 miles. Another straight line drawn from Gallup to Santa Fe reaches almost as far again. On the rough and arid surface, ridden by pony with the need constantly to avoid cavalry patrols and armed citizen-ranchers, the distance becomes considerable, even for two Apaches to cover, undetected, in ten days. Yet that is the time in which Packrat and Niño came from Seiber's cabin to the Ramona Indian school. It was, in fact, the nineteenth day of January, 1891, that the former drew rein on the juniper scarp behind the Government establishment, pointed down through the gathering, bitter cold New Mexican dusk, and said, "There it is, Niño."

The other Apache sat silently staring at the lamplit cluster of adobe buildings. There were many strong feelings in his breast at this moment, but he only nodded and said to his friend, "Yes, thank you. Isn't it strange, Packrat, how small it looks?"

"Maybe. But our minds work differently. I'm thinking how warm it looks."

"No, I mean isn't it strange how little a thing looks when at last you get right up to it? A thing you have feared and worried about for a long time? You know. Then, when you get there, it's nothing to fear or worry about at all."

"I'm still cold," insisted Packrat. "And, furthermore, you're wrong anyway. We've got plenty to worry about down there. How do you think we're going to get Chuana out of that place?"

"I'll think of something."

"Yes? Well, it better be pretty quick, if it's to come before my buttocks freeze fast to this damned saddle. By God, Niño, I never felt a wind like this at home."

"It's a Mexican wind," said Niño. "It carries a knife."

They sat their ponies, shoulders hunched, thin blankets drawn tight. Beneath them, the weary mustangs bunched their loins and stood, humpbacked, their manes and tails whipping like tattered black ensigns against the taut cords of their haunches and the ewe-bowed tendons of their scrawny necks.

At last, Niño nodded and said, "All right, come on; I know how we must do it."

"Isn't that nice," said Packrat, kicking his mount around to follow his companion's, "to have a brain like yours, Niño? Able to think of everything, and after sitting in the wind for only an hour, too."

"Schichobe," said Niño, "we all have our special strong medicine. With me it's my fine brain. With you it's that wondrous nose of yours. Who else could have smelled out this trail in ten days only?"

"Thank you, *schicho*," grimaced the pudgy San Carlos Indian. "It's a great comfort to be appreciated. It's an even greater one to know how strong we are. *Anh!* With your brains and my big nose we ought to be able to get into more trouble tonight than any Indian since Geronimo."

Niño actually laughed.

In his heart the happiness was growing with each step of the little Arizona ponies down the scarpment trail. Somewhere within that mushroom circle of friendly, twinkling lamplights ahead, Chuana waited. With his aching arms but another mile from holding her dear form once more, could a man show anything but joy over the testy comments of his faithful friend?

"Packrat," he vowed softly, "when the first man-child is born, he will bear your name."

"My God, no!" protested the other Apache. "You wouldn't do that to the poor little thing! Please, please. . . ."

But he was vastly proud, all the same, and he rode on behind his famous outlaw friend sitting very straight on his tired mustang and thinking that to have the first-born son of such blood as that of Niño and the only daughter of Eskim-in-zim called after him, was as high an honor as might come in this life to a lowly San Carlos boy with beady eyes, a short fat body and a drooping hound-dog nose.

"Now, remember," whispered Niño, "grab her quick and don't let her cry out." Packrat nodded his understanding. They lay up in the scrub behind the adobe wall of the compound, near the school well. It had been agreed that the seizing of the enemy for purposes of information had best be done by Packrat, for if the victim should recognize Niño she might well have a heart failure, or a stroke, and leave them with a body to explain and no news of Chuana, far worse. "Sure," he said, "I know my business. But I wish you had let me take that fat one. The fat ones like to be grabbed. They giggle and roll a lot but they don't fight much."

"No," said Niño, "she was too strong. Big as a horse. She might have thrown you."

"Hah! One time down in Mexico there was this Sonora girl who weighed three hundred pounds. She was like a wagon bull. Strong as Seiber. But when I got hold of her—"

"Shhh!" said Niño. "Here comes a little one. No noise, now, *cuidado!*"

"Why, that's only a *day-den,*" objected Packrat, peering hard, "only a little girl, a baby!"

"Grab her!" repeated Niño sternly, "and pull her over the wall!"

The Indian girl came gracefully down the path to the

well, carrying the earthen Zuni jug atop her head. As she put it down to draw the rusty bucket full, Packrat slid over the wall, seized her by dropping his spread blanket over her head, bundled her over his shoulder, went over the wall again and dumped her at Niño's feet.

"Get a hand over her mouth and hold it there until I have a chance to reassure her," he told Packrat.

The latter scowled, put his hand under the blanket. At once he yelped painfully and drew it back out. He damned her for an Aravaipa she-puppy, and tried again. This time he did not get bitten. As a matter of fact a pleased grin broke over his cherub's face.

"Say!" he told Niño enthusiastically, "this *day-den* isn't as little as she looked. By Yosen's big toe, she's got—"

"You fool," growled Niño, "shut up and fetch her out from under that blanket. With you yelping one minute like a stoned cur and the next cackling like an old man with a young wife, you'll have the place buzzing louder than a smoked hornet's nest before I get to ask her one question about Chuana. *Callate!*" he said, mixing the occasional Spanish word with the Apache and English which was the standard patois for agency and reservation Indians of his time. "At least let me find out if my *nah-lin* is well and strong."

Packrat grumbled something in return and pulled the not-so-little Aravaipa girl from beneath the muffling shroud of the blanket. He held her close, one hand barring her mouth, while Niño patted her tousled hair and smiled at her in a friendly way. She did not seem unduly wrought over her capture and, indeed, appeared to be enjoying the situation to some extent.

"Do you know me, little one?" asked Niño gently. "I am a friend of your people; I wish you no harm."

The girl, a bright-eyed slim thing of perhaps fifteen years, nodded vigorously and pointed to Packrat's imprisoning hand while making protesting grunts and gurgles behind the press of his grubby fingers.

"Release her," ordered Niño. "She knows my heart is good and that I won't hurt her."

"I'm not worried about how good your heart is, when it comes to getting hurt," said Packrat. "It's those damn teeth of hers that worry me. Ask her if she will not bite me again if I do as you say. I have but two thumbs and she has already ruined one of them."

Niño put the question to the girl and got another emphatic pantomime of agreement, and Packrat gingerly eased his grasp. The girl spat and rubbed her lips as though to clean them, fixing the unfortunate Packrat with a bayonet-stab of her sharp eyes.

"Don't you ever wash your hands, little fat *coche*?" she demanded. "Phew! one would imagine, from your grip, how it is like to be enfolded by a bear! Ugh!"

"Well, I like that!" stormed Packrat. "Is that what they teach you here at the school? To take a bath all the time? To keep the hands pink and the feet scrubbed? Bah! See, Niño, how quick they forget the old good ways? Don't you know, girl, that water will weaken you? You'll get sick if you keep washing all the while. That's a terrible thing! If you weren't so young, I would take you away with us."

"I'm not so young," said the girl, interested. "Where are you going?"

"Oh, don't ask me," said Packrat stiffly, "I'm just a little fat pig. You said it yourself."

"Well, I like you anyway. What's your name?"

Packrat glowed. "Na-chay-go-tah," he said.

"It's pretty," she smiled. "What does it mean?"

"Packrat," answered Niño, breaking in.

"It does not!" declared the small Apache. "That's just a name the soldiers called me at San Carlos. It has nothing to do with Na-chay-go-tah!"

"I like it even better," said the girl, patting him with her slim hand. "It fits you. I'm sorry I called you a fat little pig. You're really a fat little rat."

"By God!" cried Packrat, "I won't have it. I don't

have to sit here and listen to this ignorant Aravaipa fieldmouse call me names! I'm leaving."

Niño shoved him hard. "Sit down," he said, "and keep quiet. We've got business here. We've come a long ways and we must hurry even so." He turned to the girl. "You haven't said your name, child," he said. "How are you called among your people?"

"Many things," said the bright-eyed youngster. "But when I am good they call me Hoosh."

"Hoosh?" said Niño. "That's a strange name. It's what we call the tart red berry-fruits of the prickly pear cactus."

"That's right. Exactly why my mother named me that, too. She says I should have a name to sting the tongue and prick the hands. That is, to be like me. So it was Hoosh she chose. Don't you think it fits?"

"Yes, I'm afraid so," nodded Niño soberly. "Now, Hoosh, do you know the daughter of Eskim-in-zim who is called Chuana?"

"Of course I know her. She is practically my best friend. A little older maybe, but we like the same kinds of trouble. Why do you ask about Chuana? Who are you?"

Niño looked at her. "I thought you nodded, yes, that you knew me, when I asked you just now. Did you lie to me?"

"Only to get a breath of air," replied the girl. "That Packrat grips you like a wolftrap. I don't mind, though. I rather liked it, I think. But, no, I don't recall your face. What did you say your name was?"

He looked at her again and said quietly, "Niño."

He saw her start when he said it, and it made him unhappy that his name should have such a harsh sound even to his own people.

"Don't be afraid," he said, "please. I'm not what you hear. Those stories get tangled in the telling."

"Why, I'm not afraid!" said the girl, eyes shining, "I'm proud. Niño, here in New Mexico? All the way from Arizona? Why, that's a great thing. Chuana will just die, her poor heart will fail her, surely, when I tell her this!"

"She is here, then!" said Niño excitedly. "We have truly found her. And she is well? Not sick in any way, or hurt? They have been kind to her?"

"Sick? Her? You're talking about Chuana?"

"Yes, oh yes—!"

"Well, hardly. Not Chuana."

Niño shook his head. "She was not strong," he said. "She was never really strong. I worried a great deal."

"Well, no. Maybe she's not strong like you and me and little fat Packrat, here. But she's strong inside. Like a rifle barrel. You can't see her strength. It's rolled up inside her, do you know what I mean?"

"Yes, I know. In her heart she is *palo duro*."

"Surely, that's right; just like a hard rock. No, that's not true. Her heart is soft as soapstone. What I mean is that in her spirit she is like a rock."

"Yes, that's what you mean. I know."

Packrat stirred uneasily, casting a wary eye up toward the school buildings. "My friends," he said, "I am very awkward to do this, but I must remind you that we can't talk that girl out of those adobe barracks up there. If you could rest your tongues and exercise your brains for a moment, perhaps we could get on with the business of stealing Chuana away from here. It's just a suggestion."

"Yes, and a good one," said Niño. "Let me see, now, what would be the best way to get at her from here? Hoosh, what do you say? Whereabouts is she up there?"

The tiny Aravaipa girl shrugged. "Well," she said, "if you want to make a lot of work out of it, and perhaps get shot by the agent, or the Zuni police, why that's one thing. Go ahead up there and see what you can do. She sleeps in the big building, this way. I'll wait for you."

Niño studied her. "You haven't finished," he said. "Go on; it is us who will wait for you."

Her white teeth flashed in the windy darkness. "In that case," she smiled, "if you will stand here hidden by the wall, I will go up and get her for you and be back in ten minutes. That will include her clothes, some food stolen from the kitchen, the two army blankets from her cot, and me."

"And *what?!*" said Niño, straightening.

"Me," grinned Hoosh. "Has the wind put dust in your ears?"

"Seize her!" hissed Niño to Packrat, and dove to trap the girl himself.

But she was entirely too quick for them. Niño went sprawling empty-handed. Packrat never got off his plump hindquarters. Poised atop the low wall, Hoosh laughed happily. "If you touch me, I will cry out like a she-bear in a dog fight," she promised. "On the other hand, if you give me your word that I may go along, I will have Chuana down here before you can brush off your shirt. What do you say, Niño? And, remember, those Zuni police have shotguns. And I have a voice you will think came out of a split cannon muzzle. I'll count to three; take your time."

"Wait!" gasped Niño desperately. "For the Zuni police and their shotguns I don't give a pinch of tobacco powder. But I don't want to hear your voice. Not any more. Let me think!"

"Surely. Do that. *One—*"

"Be a good girl, Hoosh. You don't want to come with us. There will be danger. Shooting maybe."

"Almost certainly," said Hoosh. "And any minute now. *Two—*"

"Hoosh, please—!"

"Well, it's too bad, Niño. I always thought you were a great warrior. Good-bye. *Thr——*"

"Wait! All right! Have done; I'm beaten." Niño threw up his hands. "Go get Chuana. Bring the things you said. Also a few for yourself. But not many. We will be four on two horses until we can get more."

The threat carried, young Hoosh sobered for the first

time. Her slim fingers touched her forehead in salute of Indian respect. "Niño," she said, low voiced, "you will not regret this. You'll see. Hoosh never forgets."

She was gone, then, slipping off through the wind-whipped pepper trees of the garden, leaving the two Apache men alone by the low adobe wall which shut off the Ramona School from the juniper and artemesia sage and the shadowy red-dirt ribbon of the scarpment trail which led due south and west away from Santa Fe and homeward to the twisted piñons and the palos verdes of Old Arizona.

It was a lovely honeymoon trip, a little cold at first, or until they got past Gallup and started angling down into home country along the south-bearing Zuni Fork of the Little Colorado River. Then it warmed a bit. At the same time, however, the trail behind them did likewise. Pursuit, at first, had been nothing. By great luck there were no Apache police at Ramona, and the trailers among the captive Aravaipa bands of Eskim-in-zim and Chil-chu-ana at Fort Union would require a minimum of two days to get on the scene. School authorities, meanwhile, guessed that Niño had been the prime agent in the kidnap. His relationship with Chuana was well advertised and the added facet of Hoosh being included in the abduction was accepted simply as evidence of force having been the method of the crime. But assumption and certainty are different steeds and no positive identification of Niño had been arrived at up to the time that the Aravaipa scouts from Fort Union put in an appearance at Santa Fe. However, when the Apache trailers picked up the sign outside the school wall they immediately held back and went into animated conference among themselves. Shortly, they informed the white authorities in attendance—the school management as well as the sheriff and two deputies of Sandoval County (through which the scarpment trail led)—that they could make nothing of the sign except that there had been more than one kidnapper, no struggle; the mounts of the intruders had been barefooted and badly hoofsplit, that one of them was a bay with black mane, the other—there were at least two—a *grulla* with mouse-colored mane and tail, that the culprits wore *n'deh b'keh*, Apache boots, that they were one bowlegged and fairly tall, the other knock-kneed and reasonably short—that is, of the two they could point out definitely—and that it did, indeed, appear that the abductors had been Indians.

This summation delivered, the Aravaipas stood looking blandly at the frustrated white officials. No exhortations of reward or threats of punishment could induce them to add another detail. When faced with the fact that they had already supplied a great deal of pinpoint observation and could certainly have followed the trail away from the school, it being plain enough for even the Indian Bureau people to see, Eskim-in-zim, who had come with his men, suggested quietly that if the trail were so obvious to the good people of Ramona School, let them run it as far as they liked; he and his scouts had done what they could and must now return to Fort Union as they did not wish the colonel there to worry about them being away so long.

It was now clear to all that Niño *had* been outside the school wall. While the deliberate delaying tactic of the Aravaipas, who surely had guessed Niño's part in the affair before ever they set out from Fort Union, had given the kidnappers a good start, it had also established positive identification of their fellow-Apache. The telegraph keys got busy and as the fugitive lovers neared Gallup the countryside was beginning to stir against them. It was then they swung south to hit the headwaters of the Zuni, and to strike down that stream toward home. From the third day, every rider on each distant skyline became an enemy. If he could be ridden around, all right, ride around him. If he came close and there was no avoiding a meeting, then he who shot first was he that rode on alive. These were the usual terms of Niño's life since the massacre on Kelvin Grade. But he was determined that this time they should not be forced upon him. This time, for the sake of Chuana and Hoosh and his dear friend Packrat, he must not let them put him in a place from which his only escape lay in killing those between him and freedom.

It was a deadly game. But with the skills and instincts sharpened by the two long years he had already played to its rules, Niño was able to lead his followers out of New Mexico without firing a shot. It was when he had gotten them a hundred miles into Arizona, safely onto the San Carlos Reservation and headed for home, that instinct, skill and rare Apache luck ran out.

The lieutenant was not young. Neither was he inexperienced. He had been in the territories six years. Twice passed over for his captaincy, twice reprimanded for overzealous care of prisoners in the field, he was not burning to make a poor record better, but only to finish the present tour and retire with his two bars. He was, in a word, the wrong officer to be coming down the Fort Apache wagon-road above Kinishba Ruin with Sergeant Rice, Corporal Schmidtlap, two San Carlos scouts and ten men of E Troop, Third Cavalry, at sundown of February 2, 1891.

The patrol was trail-weary. It had chased a futile week after a band of Mase's Mexican Apaches up from Sonora to kill a few fat beeves on the American side. The Indians had made fools of the troops as they did each time a cross-grained officer of Beacham's type ordered a pursuit against the advice of his own Apaches. In this case Beacham had overruled two of the best, accusing them of selling out to their wild cousins and ordering them put in arrest for the return journey. Thus he had not only his ten troopers and two noncoms staring holes between his shoulderblades, but his brace of Apache trackers, as well.

In addition, with their feet tied under their horses' bellies, their hands manacled and their mounts ignominiously neck-roped to the crupper strap of the troop's lone packmule, Josh and Nosey were in no position, much less mood, to render their usual services to overage Lieutenant J.D.E. Beacham.

It was Corporal Schmidtlap who saw the dead steer. The animal lay a pistol shot off the road, and in such a posture that it suggested something rather than disease or natural accident as the manner of its going.

"Lieutenant," he said, "that beef yonder's been fresh killed."

Sergeant Rice and Beacham pulled in their mounts. Rice waved back the halt to the column.

"Schmidtlap's right, sir," he said. "We'd best watch it. There's apt to be 'Paches about."

Beacham grimaced. "This close to the fort?" he scowled. "Don't be ridiculous."

Rice held tight. "Could be that's their thinking, sir, to come in so close we'd never think to look for them. I'd like to ride over and see."

Beacham frowned again, but nodded. "Corporal," he said to Schmidtlap, "you go. Rice, tell the men to stay mounted. We're short on daylight. Hop it, Schmidtlap."

The latter turned his horse and rode toward the downed steer. As he neared it, an Indian rose up from behind its body, butcherknife in hand. Schmidtlap was so surprised he simply pulled up his mount and sat there. Moreover, he drew the line at shooting squaws, a moral weakness which was to repay him dearly before another day. Behind him, Lieutenant James Beacham shared no such restraints.

"Pull away, you damned fool!" he shouted. "You're blocking our line of fire!" Then, wildly, to Rice. "Goddamn it, Sergeant, don't just sit there! Shoot!"

"Sir!" said Rice desperately, "it's a woman."

"It's an Apache!" blazed Beacham, "and that's an order I gave you. Carry it out!"

"Yes, sir," said Sergeant Rice, and fired his Spencer high and wide of the Indian woman.

The shot broke the glaze of fear which had been holding the trapped squaw motionless. Wheeling, she ran swiftly back over the lip of a shallow arroyo behind her.

"After her!" yelled Beacham to his troopers at large. "Don't let her get away!"

There was a moment's hesitation, then three or four of the younger men started after Rice, who had loped off in pursuit of the woman following his deliberately missed shot at her. The remainder of the troopers fell in belatedly, hardly urging their worn horses to the work. Rice held up at the edge of the arroyo looking for the vanished squaw. The men came up behind him and, as they did, Josh and Nosey came up to Beacham, who was still shouting orders and epithets at his command, while making no great effort to join its members in the chase.

"Lieutenant," said Josh, "you had better call in the men. That was Chuana behind that steer. You know, Niño's girl. He may be near."

"What?! Niño? My God—!" He spurred his mount toward the arroyo. "Wait, wait!" he yelled at Rice, just starting his horse down into the depression. "Hold off, Josh says we may have Niño cornered!"

Josh had said no such thing, but Beacham was suddenly smelling Apache blood and his captain's bars. If they could run the woman back to her sweetheart, they would have a prize second only to Lieutenant Gatewood's achievement in rounding up Geronimo. They mustn't shoot her now whatever they did, but neither must they let her rest or quit running long enough to think.

"Keep after her!" he told Rice, sliding his horse up to the latter's, "but fire high. Just keep her rolling-eyed and running. She'll lead us right to him, if he's around. Come on! By God, there'll be a promotion in this for you, too, Rice. Forward, ho—!"

The sweep of gauntlet and spin of horshflesh with which he led off the pursuit would have done credit to George Armstrong Custer. And so would the generalship impelling the flourish. Rice, an old soldier and hence badly frightened at the prospect of jumping Niño with only ten tired men, nonetheless rode jump for jump behind his excited officer. Schmidtlap, a less courageous, less dedicated man, let the three forward troopers dash by him, then followed with checked rein at the head of the remaining seven. The latter appeared satisfied with the gait, circumstances considered. Niño may have been out of sight for a year—he had scarcely been out of mind.

Ahead, the arroyo closed in. It would pass one rider for a distance of a furlong. Beyond that, it flared out to become a grassy flat dotted with large boulders and walled in by the flanks of the widened arroyo. Beacham, shouting in the lead, burst into this arena looking for the Aravaipa girl, Chuana. He found, instead, another Apache. A San Carlos. Medium dark and leanly handsome for a member of his squat, large-headed race. Very impressive, too, with his coarse black hair held in by its scarlet headcloth, his patched U.S. cavalry shirt adorned by its tattered yellow chevrons, his leather, full-length leggins and high *n'deh b'keh*, Apache moccasin boots. And, oh yes, with his new Model 1886 Winchester held at hip-level and swung to cover the dusty tunic of Lieutenant J.D.E. Beacham.

Niño shot the officer two times, head and chest. Sgt. Rice, riding next, could not check his mount. Given no choice, Niño shot him also. But only once. The three troopers, hearing the firing, jammed their horses in a tangle at the opening of the arena. Before they could get them separated and spurred for the sloping sides of the arroyo, each had taken a 44-40 through the body; two in fleshy, superficial parts, the third a mortal hit slanting through both kidneys. As the last of them did get his mount up the bank, Schmidtlap tried desperately to halt and turn his mount in the narrow passage. But the animal had powder-smoke in its nostrils and the sounds of battle in its ears. It was an old Third Cavalry campaigner, and it took its hapless rider right on out into the Apache's fire. Niño, badly hurried, missed his shot, the bullet going low and dropping the horse. But the fall pinned the soldier's left foot and Niño ran forward for the Apache finish.

Raising the steelshod butt of his carbine to crush the soldier's skull, he caught himself in mid-swing, stopped the blow inches short of the pale, unprotected face beneath him.

"I'm sorry," he said. "In this bad light, I didn't see it was you."

With these words, he leaped over Schmidtlap's horse and ran crouchingly up the wall of the arroyo to get above the remaining troopers on the far side of the narrows. He was back before the shaken corporal's head cleared.

"They've gone," he said. "All running like rabbits for the old ruins over there at Kinishba. Lie quiet there and I will lift the saddle. When I do, see if you can get your leg out. All right?"

Schmidtlap, speechless with fear, nodded. Niño put his rawhide muscle to the lift. Feeling the pressure ease, the corporal withdrew his leg and rolled free.

"Thank you," he said, weak voiced, and sat watching the Apache, still livid with fright.

"It's me who thanks you," answered Niño. "You could have shot my woman over there and you wouldn't do it."

"I couldn't," said Schmidtlap. Then haltingly. "Is she all right? Did they hit her?"

Niño shook his head. "No, they didn't hit her. She got away with my other friends, while I stayed to talk with your lieutenant. I know him." He nodded to the dead Beacham. "He's no good. But I'm sorry about the sergeant. He was only a soldier. Only doing what he was told. I know how that is. You tell them at Fort Apache that Niño is sorry about the sergeant."

"You're letting me go?" said Schmidtlap unbelievingly.

Niño nodded. The soldier looked around uncertainly,

eyes coming to rest on Sergeant Rice's body. "You're sure about him?" he asked. "He don't look bad hit. Maybe—"

"In the heart," said Niño. "I had no time to be careful; I had to shoot him in the center." He glanced around at the gathering dusk. "You can walk to your friends," he said quickly. "We need these two horses, my friends and me." He took up the reins of Rice's mount, swung up on Beacham's fine sorrel. "You tell Josh and Nosey they were smart to sit still and say nothing just now," he added. "Tell them they will be even smarter if they keep doing the same thing. Can you walk all right?"

Schmidtlap tried a gingerly step or two, nodded again.

"Good," grunted the Apache. "Now we both go."

He had turned the horses and kicked them into a gallop before the soldier could reply. Now the latter ran a pointless few feet after him and called out, "Thank you; thank you very much." Then he stopped and stood still, feeling foolish, and still very much afraid. "My God," he said half aloud, "that was him; that was *Niño. . . !*"

6

They rode thirty miles that night. At dawn they came to Carrizo Creek. Pulling in his pony, Packrat said, "This is the place I told you of; we will be safe here for today."

"Yes," said Niño, "I remember it now. My father

took me here one time hunting beaver. There's a trail follows the stream up to Wildhorse Lake, am I right?"

"Very right, yes. It's that trail I'm thinking of. We can talk about it after we get the women to rest."

Niño nodded. The horses, their original four stolen enroute from New Mexico, had traveled seventy miles the past twenty-four hours. The strong-looking cavalry horses had gone but the thirty from Kinishba Ruin, yet were more wasted than the tough mustangs. Rest was indeed imperative.

"Chuana," he said to the slim girl beside him, "you and Hoosh ride on down. We will follow."

Chuana said nothing, only clucked to her pony and put it down the remainder of the trail to creekside. Hoosh followed next, then Packrat, with Niño last.

It was simple Apache custom. In any situation where the possibility of surprise obtained, the squaws went in first to draw the fire. In this instance only the rush of the creekwater greeted Chuana and Hoosh, and Niño, after a final searching look at the backtrail, sent Beacham's sorrel down the brief incline to the cover of desert cottonwood growing thinly at stream's edge. The fact it was winter and the trees denuded did not deny the advantage of camouflage provided by the pattern of the tangled bare limbs. Four Indians and six horses could disappear under such a mixture of light and shadow, defying separation and discovery save by other Indians. And then only from a very close viewpoint. Since the nearest of these was the ring of low hills they had come through five miles south and east, Niño felt adequately secure.

Hoosh and Chuana, reared in the old ways among the Aravaipas, soon had a snug camp made. It was in under a forty-foot bluff of weathered lime. The overhang was deep enough to provide almost a cave. Its ceiling was black with the fires of centuries of Indian parties stopping here, and its effect of smoke dispersion so obviously well-tried and safe that Niño granted permission for a small blaze to be lit. It was their first since the previous day's breakfast and it was a good and welcome thing to see.

All four Indians gathered around its glowing cheer, after Niño and Packrat had studied the escape of the smoke and decided it was acceptable. Nothing in life was without risk for them, as long as they clung to their slender leader. They understood this, Packrat best of all, and while they were not happy over it, neither did they allow it to obtrude on the small pleasures of the hour.

Behind them lay two dead and one dying soldier. One of the killed was an officer. Two more soldiers had been wounded, seven put to shameful, broken flight. All this to the account of one Indian—Niño. Heretofore, living witnesses against the Mad Wolf of the San Carlos had been wanting. Now there were seven for sure, nine if the two wounded troopers recovered, ten if the corporal spared by Niño repaid the charity with official testimony.

This was a grim thing, even for a people born and reared in an atmosphere of grim things. They were still on San Carlos Reservation, up in the extreme northwest corner of it. They had covered their trail well, but Josh and Nosey had seen where it started and were the best trailers, barring Niño and Packrat, in the whole country. They would be brought back to the scene by the soldiers from Fort Apache and would not refuse to follow the tracks of their old friends. They did not know that Packrat was the fourth Indian of the fugitives from the Kinishba slaughter, but they would find it out, sooner or later, if the fat brave stayed with Niño and the squaws.

No, theirs was not a happy situation there in the limestone overhang beside Carrizo Creek. But they were Apaches. Tomorrow's trouble would be taken tomorrow; today's enjoyments embraced today.

So breakfast was a brief time of forgetfulness for the two men, smiles, light talk and some few teasing caresses from the young Aravaipa girls. But with food and warmth, and with windfree shelter, fatigue replaced frivolity very quickly. Soon Chuana was asleep, Packrat nodding, even Niño beginning to yawn.

"Hoosh," he said, "you are the strongest. Will you watch first?"

"For you, Niño," said the tiny girl, "I would watch always. Sleep well. I won't fail you."

Niño looked at her a moment, feeling something he could not name, but which made him uneasy at the same time it reassured him. "I believe you, Hoosh," he nodded finally, and lay down. She watched him until his breathing slowed and became deep. Then she glanced at Packrat and Chuana. Both were turned peacefully on their sides. She put her hands to Niño's face, lingeringly let the slim fingers trace its weary lines. Then she bent swiftly and kissed him on the lips. He stirred and Hoosh smiled and put her blanket over him and pulled it close and went to sit, high-chinned and proud, in the entranceway until sundown.

She was still there, still alertly watching the backtrail, when twilight stole over the ragged peaks of the Mazatzals to the west and Packrat awoke with a guilty start and growled, "Eh, what the devil? Day's end already and no one called me?"

Brightening visibly when he saw his shapely trailmate on guard at the opening, he added beamingly, "Ah, Hoosh! there you are! And did you rest well, Little One—?"

Hoosh nodded, a strange softness in her voice.

"Wonderfully well!" she sighed, and lay down and was asleep before the hopefully solicitous Packrat could utter another amorous commonplace, or, indeed, think of one.

The night was down and they would have to travel soon. Both sat yet a while longer, smoking their cornshuck *cigarillos*. It was Niño who spoke first.

"Well, friend," he said, "we have come to another hard parting, I think."

Packrat, glancing over the edge of the overhang to see that the women, busy with the packing below, were not listening, nodded. "I was thinking the same thing," he said.

"I want to thank you," said Niño. "I could never have done it without your help."

"Nonsense, you could have done it easily."

"Chuana would have been captured, killed perhaps, and I dead, certainly, had you not been there to lead away the women yesterday."

"Bah, it was nothing."

"You showed me the way to the school. You stayed with me all the way back. Even when the soldiers came upon us and Josh and Nosey were with them to identify you if they should have seen you, you would not leave me. You know what would have happened to you if they had caught sight of you. You would have been shot when captured."

"Well, what of it? I have been chasing Apaches for them ten years. At any time I might have been shot."

"It's true, but it's different."

"How different?"

"One may be shot with honor, or without it."

"Bah! Honor belongs to the old days, Niño. There is no honor any more. Either you fight with the soldiers or against them. One way is no better than the other."

"Yes it is, my friend." Niño paused, looking again into the deepening night. His hand went unconsciously to the chevrons on his sleeve. "If I must die, I would rather die a soldier than to die out in the rocks like a horse with a broken leg, or a starving dog with no master's hand to touch him, or kind voice to say good-bye to him."

Packrat shivered. "What a way to talk!" he grumbled. "You sound as though you were already *dah-eh-sah*, already dead. That's enough of that. You have your woman with you, good horses, a fine rifle, field glasses, canteens, blankets, a long start on the soldiers and my wedding present. What more could you ask?"

Niño's dry smile twisted across his lips. "Your wedding present?" he said. "Now that interests me. Tell me about it, and then we must go. It's getting late."

"It's about your going that my present concerns. I want you to listen very carefully. All right?"

"Yes, go on."

"Well, do you recall that I was born in Verde Valley, over near Tuzigoot?"

"Yes, of course."

"Also that I am some years older than yourself?"

"I recall these things, yes, but what has your age to do with anything?"

"Just that I was old enough, when I lived over there, to remember many things. One of them was that big ruin of the cliff people over on Beaver Creek."

"You mean the one the soldiers from Camp Verde used to call Montezuma's Castle?"

"That's the one."

"Well, what about it?"

"First, there are no more soldiers at Camp Verde. They left last year and did not go back. Is that not right?"

"Yes, but what of it? Surely you're not suggesting that we hide in Camp Verde!"

"No, I'm suggesting you honeymoon in Montezuma's Castle. If you're careful to keep a good watch from the cliff and to do your hunting a long ways from there, so that the gun shots won't be heard by passers along the Verde, I think you can winter there like a king and queen of the old ones. What do you think?"

Niño didn't know what to think. He had never seen the ruins on Beaver Creek. His people had been driven by the Army out of the Verde Valley onto the arid San Carlos before his birth, and they had shown a reluctance to go back to the old home, or even to talk about it. So only the older ones, like Packrat, had any useful memories of the verdant river and its canyoned tributaries. Yet the words of Packrat struck a shaft of instinct deep into him. Somehow he knew the little San Carlos scout had just said something very important.

"Schichobe," he replied, "I don't know what to think. But my spirit says to trust your word. I have killed an officer and a sergeant and wounded three soldiers, and I think one of them will die from the way he slumped over his horse's withers going up out of the arroyo. I know I must hide, and I don't know where. If I try to get through to Mexico and join Massai and the others down on the Sierra Madre, I will take a great chance of harming Chuana. They will be watching every trail and all the Apache scouts will be crawling the secret ways in between the trails. They will shoot her as quickly as they will me, either the scouts or soldiers. I don't know what to do."

"I have just told you, *schichobe.*" Packrat looked over the edge once more, checking the women. Continuing, he lowered his voice. "Now, listen, the country south of us will be sealed off. But north, the way we're going, there's a chance. Especially the way I have it figured out for my wedding present. Are you listening, Niño?"

"Yes, yes," answered his companion, "I am just watching to be sure the women don't hear. We don't want to frighten them."

"No," said Packrat, "nor to let them in on our plans either. That Hoosh must go back with me, and she talks too much. She must not know where you and Chuana are going. You agree?"

"Yes, go ahead."

"All right, here is the whole thing."

Quickly he laid it out, Niño nodding wordlessly as he went along. It was a bold plan but the best one to be had. Hoosh, after her daylong, sleepless vigil, and now with the work of packing, would be dead tired. They would tell her the start would not be made until midnight, and persuade her to lie down and sleep. As soon as she was breathing deep, Niño and Chuana would leave. Packrat would stay with Hoosh, letting her sleep as long as nature demanded. When she awoke, he would tell her that Niño and Chuana had fled in the night, and while he, too, drowsed. They, he and Hoosh, would then set out for San Carlos. After some days of hiding on Packrat's *rancheria* below Chutanay Mesa, the Aravaipa girl would be smuggled onto another *rancheria* and then another—all of friends who could be trusted—until all trace of her incoming trail with Packrat would be hopelessly tangled, faded, erased. Then she would show up at the Agency office one fine morning and say she was Hoosh, the captive of Niño, escaped at last and come, after unmentionable hardships, up out of the Mexican Sierra, whence Niño had taken her and the other girl, Chuana.

There was always the risk, of course, that Hoosh would one time say the wrong thing to the wrong person. But by then there would be no chance of picking up Niño's trail from Carrizo Creek. The snows of winter would have covered it in the high places, and the rains of spring washed it out in the low. Moreover, there was no better way. Niño could accept Packrat's wedding gift of Montezuma's Castle or he could refuse it and flee from this camp by his own direction. That direction would have to be Mexico. He could not wander at large the winter through in Arizona. The Kinishba killings had assured that. The thin Apache youth did not take overlong with his decision.

"Packrat," he said, after the final, stretching silence, "how do I get there from this place?"

They swung on northward, following Carrizo Creek. Moving only by night and being painstaking to cover every hoofprint of their passing, they were a full week in reaching the mouth of Beaver Creek on the Verde, a hundred miles arrowflight, from the overhang cave on the Carrizo.

It was nearing dawn of the seventh night when Niño drew rein at the Beaver confluence. Peering up the tributary stream, then at the paling sky to the east, he spoke softly to Chuana.

"We are nearly there now. Packrat said it was but three miles from here. Do you want to go on?"

The Aravaipa girl nodded sleepily. "If you say so, Niño," she replied. "I am very tired."

"So am I, *nah-lin*." He still called her by the Apache name for the young unmarried woman. On the trail, when there is imminent danger of a fight, the dedicated Indian does not consort with his women. It was the Old Law. Mostly it meant nothing since the corruptive coming of the white man, but some Indians kept the faith still. Niño was of these. "We will go on up the creek," he said. "It promises better cover than we have here along the river, and we will be in time to see our new home by the sunrise. That's always a good sign."

"Yes," said Chuana, "I would like that."

They went on, going the first mile through the creek bed. The water, winter-low, was no deeper than their stirrups, even in the pools. Yet it was running free, not stagnant or dry intermittently, as with so many Arizona small streams before the spring melt, and they were able to hide their trail beautifully. When, finally, the roughening terrain required them to leave the bed, they were able to do so on a rocky sheet of Cenozoic limestone which held the splashings of the creekwater that followed them out of the stream only long enough for the dry air and cool morning breeze to dry them away. Then there remained no sign at all, either at their leaving of the Verde, or the Beaver, and they came, shortly, to their first sight of Montezuma's Castle as Niño had hoped—with the sun just breaking over the Mogollon Plateau to the East.

They sat their ponies, struck speechless.

The sight of the ancient marvel of the Pueblos, viewed as they were viewing it, through a lacy frame of Arizona sycamore limbs, yellow-bloomed desert holly, winter-brown velvet ash and gray mesquite boughs, was enough to make even a white man pause. For Indians who loved the land and looked to nature as the governing force of all things, plant and animal, and who saw the mystery and the wonder of the power of Creation in even so simple a work as the petal of a cactus rose or the wispy down of a milkweed thistle, the impact of the towering white limestone "city in the sky" was overwhelming.

Glancing at Chuana, Niño saw that she was crying. He looked quickly away, back at the cliff, not wanting her to know he had seen her tears. When any Indian cries it is a rare thing. When an Apache cries it is a matter of absolute tabu, a personal emotion sacred to the individual. Another Apache honors it in silence and he never interrupts it. Niño sat waiting for the woman who Hoosh had said was so "hard inside." When she had recovered herself they would talk.

Meanwhile, Niño studied the dazzling face of the great white cliff before them; and felt a lump grow in his own throat, and the constriction of the muscles about his own eyecorners grow tight. This was a thing of his native red kind, built by the people before his people, a half a thousand winters ago. This was a thing the red man had done. And where, in all the world, was there a thing to compare with it which the white man had done?

Niño did not know. But he could not believe, in this first vision of the lofty ruin, that the white man had ever wrought so wondrous a work. It filled him with awe for its dizzying perch upon the sheer face of the canyon wall, and for the marvel of its primitive engineering and the incredible facts of its stone-by-stone construction by a people who had neither machinery nor metal tools. But it filled him more with the simple pride of its being an *Indian* thing. Something of *his* people. A monument to show all who might come this way in the next half a thousand winters, that here the *red man* had paused and left *his* mark.

In silence, Niño uncased his field glasses.

He was curious both for a closer view of the pueblo's

trails, ladders, approaches, intact rooms and various inhabitable levels, as well as to be sure the eternal stillness of the place was not a lie, that it did not, in fact, shroud some previous tenant now looking back across the Beaver at him and his slender bride.

The castle sat a hundred feet above the valley floor, fitted so skillfully and securely into its cliff-pocket that it had stood virtually undamaged by the elements for all of the 500 years since its last known dwellers had departed its twenty narrow rooms. It faced broadly south, looking over the valley of the Beaver, so that now, in midwinter, the sun was upon it nearly the entire day. By equally important token, Niño knew that in the blazing heat of the Verde summer, the cliff face would be in almost total shadow for the daylight hours. Below the castle, reaching from it to ground level, were a series of ledges and ladders and individual rooms and isolated apartments and eyries and lookouts and work levels which literally honeycombed the canyon wall. Wherever a stratum of the softer clays, silts and conglomerate pebbles had eroded out of the basic limestone to provide a shelf, the ancients had cleared a walkway or constructed a shelter. No aperture bigger than the huddled body of a child had been left undeveloped for the community need. The result left Niño's Apache imagination afire with wonder and excitement.

Through the glasses he could measure the butts of the sycamore logs protruding from the clay mortar of the very highest structures. They were ten and even twelve inches in diameter, and who knew how long? How in Yosen's name had the Pueblos hauled them a hundred feet and more up the sheer cliff? Or the base stones of some of the apartments—great hulking slabs and chunks of valley floor rock brought from below—by what means? Those people could have had no more than ropes of grass or yucca fibre and stone hammers and simple wooden sapling-levers with which to fell and bring up from the creek bed those great roof timbers and foundation stones. And the tens of thousands of grass baskets of clay and sand mortar with which each wall was cemented, small stone by small stone, these all must have also come up the cliff face by hand-power.

How?

Niño shook his head, and the first pride he had felt was now compounded a hundredfold.

Moving the glasses along the cliff and lowering them in search of possible dwellings at a lesser level than the castle, he noted what had been another complete five-story pueblo, possibly eighty or ninety paces upstream, which appeared to have been gutted by fire in some past century. Its log ceilings destroyed, the rain had come in and, with the passage of time and weakening of the instable cliff by the intense heat of the fire, had peeled the entire pueblo from its niche and spilled it at the base of the canyon wall. Above this charred heap of rubble a lone ladder was still in place, reaching to a ledge which appeared to front a natural cave in the limestone.

Niño took down the glasses to study the place with the naked eye.

The more he looked, the better he was pleased with what he saw.

The access to the ledge which supported the foot of the ladder seemed at first glance to be impassable. Only detailed study with the glass showed the narrow, camouflaged track which climbed to it from stream level. Along the ladder ledge, another trail, invisible to the unsupported or casual eye, ran along the face of the parent cliff a quarter of a mile, terminating in a deep cleft which led, via a detritus-filled bottom, by steep but open going, back again to the valley floor. Yet so jammed with desert willow, cottonwood, sycamore and mesquite growth were both the exit cleft and the creek's bottomland where the cleft came down to it, that no eye but that of an Indian, and then aided by a good U.S. cavalry glass, could have detected even the suspicion of an escape route in this direction.

The complete picture of the lone-laddered cave, apart and yet an immediate part of the major castle, as well as of the collapsed five-story lesser pueblo, was so perfectly innocent and unlikely as a place of dwelling, amid all the other and more obvious opportunities in the great silent city on the sunlit wall, that Niño knew, within seconds of his first glassing, that here was not only a snug, warm-porched honeymoon retreat but a wolf-lonely, escape-hatched outlaw's lair, as well. And he knew, when he lowered the glasses and looked again at Chuana, that the wedding gift of Packrat was finer than all the silver of the Spaniard, the gold of the Aztec, the turquoise of the Navajo, or the iron dollars of the U.S. Army. Yet all he said to her was, "Come on, we will cross over and make camp." And all she answered to him was a nod and a smile and a soft word to her tired pony. The little animal flicked its ears and whickered in response and, together with Niño's dust-caked roan, went forward into the Beaver Creek shallows, and splashing on through them toward the glistening white and perpendicular stillness of Montezuma's Castle.

They chose the cave upon closer inspection. It was thirty feet deep, fifteen wide. It consisted of the flaring outer portion, which Niño called their sunporch, and a cozy inner room entered by a narrowed passageway in the limestone barely tall enough to pass a bent figure. The inner room, by a freak of nature, had a water-cut fissure in the ceiling which, while it had centuries ago ceased to drip moisture, now served as an ideal air vent and smoke issuance. Yet, in the latter capacity, as they found, so diverse were its hidden features through the great cliff, that no outer trace of the escaping heat and smoke could be detected.

Beneath this natural chimney, the ancients had built a stone firepit. The floor of the room was level and built up four inches over its stone base with fine-sifted river sand, smooth and white-pink as any palace paving. The winter's firewood of the last inhabitant, together with his stone *metates* for grinding corn, his clay *ollas* for the storage of water, his stone hoes, axes, adzes, *manos* (corn smashers) and eating bowls were all neatly arranged along the various niches and crevices in the warm white walls of the inner room. On these walls the brightly painted pictographs of the Pueblos, placed on sections of the base-rock smoothed with lime-plaster, showed as cheerfully fresh and artful as though the pigment were scarcely dry. The charred pieces of half-burned wood lying in the firepit seemed almost to still be wisping smoke. At the edge of the pit, two stone eating dishes and a water vessel stood placed for the final meal. To Niño and Chuana, standing entranced in the low opening of the inner chamber, it appeared as though their predecessor couple had left the room not ten minutes gone. Yet both the young Apaches knew, from the tribal stories of these vanished kinsmen, that those supper dishes and that half-burned fire had been waiting half a thousand years for the people who had left them there and disappeared forever in the murky nowhere of fifteenth-century legend.

Chuana shivered and drew closer to Niño. He shielded her willingly, spoke low-voiced and with one of his rare slow smiles. "It's only the chill of a long time past," he said. "Ten minutes of a good fire will chase it away. Come, you'll see."

He moved to the center of the room, and struck and held aloft toward the ceiling crevice a sulphur match. The puff of fume emitted by the ignited wood drifted at once and sharply upward. "Ah ha!" he exclaimed, "it is as I thought. Now, watch—" He began to replace the charred kindling in the firepit, but Chuana moved quickly forward, her smile lighting the dimness of the cavern-room. "Is that a warrior's work to do?" she asked, placing her slim hand on his shoulder. "What am I, Niño? Your woman or your guest?"

Niño laughed joyfully. And Chuana, pleased with the sound and with the look of happiness which came suddenly to the dark face where tragedy dwelled so often and so deeply, laughed with him. Her clear voice rang beautifully in the limestone chamber, echoed like a bell from the flared walls of the sunporch. They looked at one another, dark eyes burning, young bodies suddenly robbed of weariness and fear. They embraced, standing.

It was the first full contact of their forms in all the time since Niño had come to sit in courtship outside her father's wickiup. Chuana felt weak. She began to tremble. Putting her arms more tightly about Niño's neck, she pressed forward into him, moving instinctively. He stiffened, drew a little away from her.

"No," he said resolutely, "not here. Come—"

They went out onto the warmth and morning brilliance of the sunporch. They had placed there, upon first climbing to the level, their blanket rolls and supply bags. Niño stepped past these to the ladderhead. Below, in the winter-cured rich hay of the creek bottom, he saw the horses grazing peacefully. Up- and down-canyon nothing stirred which should not. A brown hawk on the morning hunt hung high over the outer valley of the Verde. Along the Beaver, a gray fox lapped at stream's edge two hundred yards off. A hundred yards in the other direction a covey of fat Mexican quail whistled cheerily to a second hatch of cousins across the creek. Niño nodded to himself, pulled the ladder up to the cave-bench level. Stowing it, he picked up the blanket rolls and spread them in the full glow of the sun at the base of the rear porch wall. It was as warm there as in the snuggest wickiup. As safe as the heart of the Sonora Sierra. As still and drowsy and inviting as the softest bed of robes and furs.

Chuana followed him without order. She moved her deft hands swiftly about their work with the fastenings of her trail clothing. When Niño straightened and turned, she was waiting for him.

He took the slim, bare body in his arms. He was gentle with her, not fierce. Easy and careful and controlled as he was, however, he did not lack sureness with her. This was his woman. They were safe. They had waited a very long while. Yet it was *enthlay-sitdaou*, the old Apache law of iron restraint, that a man be not like an animal with his young virgin bride, but like a man.

When the quiet time came, when the wanting and the hunger were done, and when the stillness and the sun and the call of the quail in the canyon were all that remained to ease their lovers' sleep, Chuana knew the wisdom and the peace and the truth of that old law.

7

The winter went swiftly. Hunting was good, with only enough snow on the higher places to track the deer. Niño shot much game and Chuana, accompanying him through the first months, cared for it in the field. They brought home both meat and skin and fur to their cavern ledge above the Beaver. By early spring the place was hung and draped and carpeted with soft-tanned deerhides and lush, glossy-pelted bearskins. These furnishings, together with the housekeeping vessels of the ancients, made the cave the best home either Apache had known.

Water of the clearest, coldest and most delicious kind flowed at their doorstep. Food in sufficiency was to be had for the seeking, both in the farther hills and in the canyon below. No shooting was done here, of course, but Chuana's skill with the set-snare and the box-trap and the beaver-stick kept them in succulent small game through those rare times when venison or antelope or bearsteaks were not hanging in the cavern cooler-niche. Grass for the two horses—three, now that the mare had dropped a wobbly foal in late April—grew everywhere on both sides of the Beaver and when that failed there was always mustang forage budding among the many trees and bushes of the bottomland.

The life, even with the terms of constant vigilance and strict discipline of movement demanded by Niño's crime, was a richly rewarding one.

To Niño it was a constant revelation of Chuana's soft sweetness and love. Yes, and of her considerable ableness to make a home in other ways. Still, she was a strange girl. Not strong and not of the old ways in her mind, she did not hate the whites, or the soldiers, and the savagery of some of her own people dismayed her. As to Niño's past, she never spoke. But he knew that it worried her at heart, and that the fear of living as a hunted thing was gnawing at her even when she smiled and denied it to him. Yet they were happy. As happy as Niño had been in his life. As happy as those dear days he could remember when he was the pet and the mascot of the tough old soldiers at San Carlos, and those other, later good days when he stood first at Al Seiber's side of all Apache scouts in Arizona.

Some of the times that spring, when it was cold and blustery and the rain was winnowing up the canyon from the outer valley of the Verde, Niño went and sat upon the ledge and watched out to the east and south, down toward the Gila and the San Carlos, and felt lonely and sad and restless in his spirit. It was these times that he thought of Seiber. And thought, too, of the wasted life he had squandered when he let Lizard and the other bad ones talk him into facing his big white friend in anger and deceit that long-ago day at the reservation.

Then, truly, his heart sank.

Had he gone to Seiber as a boy to his father, all would have been different today. Those brave chevrons on the ragged shirt would not be soiled and torn and raveled as they now were. They would still be bright and clean and new. They would still say that he was a soldier of the Third U.S. Cavalry, and they would say, even more importantly, that he and Chuana could live as human beings among their kin, and that when the little one came he could go to the post and be praised and petted and admired and made much of by the soldiers, even as his father before him. And, too, when his time came he could also wear the chevrons and serve under the flag of the regiment and the big flag, too, with its white stars and red stripes. But now—now what? What of Niño and what of Chuana and what of the baby growing in Chuana's belly?

Nothing.

Yosen had been good. He had given them this winter and this spring safe in the white bosom of Montezuma's Castle. He had let their love be strong. He had let it spring also to seed, so that Niño, when at last and inevitably the soldiers should shoot him, would not be forgotten among his people. This was good, and Niño was grateful for it. Yet beyond this spring what waited for him and his wife and his unborn child?

Again, nothing.

It was, Niño tried to think at these depressing times, the fault of Seiber having turned upon him at the Fish Creek cabin, which had cast his life into the dark channel it now coursed, and from which it could never turn aside.

Had the German scout let him come in when he gave the cactus owl signal, who could say what happier things would now surround Niño? But that his old friend should answer to the signal and then try to kill him when he showed himself; this was the hurt which had no healing. In vain had his comrade Packrat argued that it could not have been Seiber who fired upon them; that Seiber would never stoop to such cowardly tricks; that Seiber had shown himself many times ready to risk all he owned, even his reputation, that he might help his friend, Niño, to lift from his own name the ugly stain which it did not deserve. But Niño could not believe it. Packrat had said Seiber wanted to see him. Packrat had led him to where Seiber lived. Their greeting had been deadly bullets fired in the gray dawn. Niño never doubted Packrat for that terrible surprise, but he would never trust Seiber again after it. Or so he attempted to tell himself those homesick times when the rain or thin snow spat down the canyon of the Beaver and he sat upon the limestone ledge of his cavern lair in Montezuma's cliff with his heart as heavy as the cold winter air about him.

In the end he could not convince his spirit of Seiber's guilt. After leaving Fish Creek and following the first hot debate with Packrat, they had not again discussed the matter. But as winter now wore away and spring drew on, he thought more and more about the kindly German scout who had befriended him before all other whites. And he thought more and more that Packrat had been right, and that Al Seiber could not have fired at the Apache boy he had called the finest trailer in all the Southwest and upon whom he had conferred the very high honor of making him the youngest Indian ever to serve with the regular U.S. Army.

But the restoration of faith came too late. It came too late by one dead officer and one dead sergeant and one dying soldier at the cavalry ambush at Kinishba Ruin. And it came too late by two other wounded soldiers and the saddle-pinned corporal who had been spared and who would be able to testify in a military inquiry as to the positive identity of the lone Apache renegade who had stood in the trail at Dead Steer Arroyo and shot to death the officer and the sergeant, and mortally wounded the soldier who stayed on his horse.

That Apache was Niño.

There could be no turning to Al Seiber now. Not now and not ever again. Neither could there be any further placing of the blame for his own evil deeds upon the quiet, calm-eyed Chief of Scouts. Niño had done what he had done. It was he who must pay for it.

The trail ahead from this happy resting place in Beaver Creek Canyon had been laid by his own bloody *n'deb b'keh*. It led precisely to where Seiber had always said it must lead if he persisted in his wild outlaw ways: it led to nowhere.

These grim thoughts of the gray days thawed gradually as the ground-frost disappeared from the bottomland swales and the rim ice melted from the bedrock potholes along the Beaver. Spring turned, summer came on apace; Chuana's belly grew, Niño's dark presciences retreated.

No one came to the canyon, or even to the rim above. Occasionally a party passed along the Verde trail going to Prescott or to Tuzigoot or to Payson, but none turned aside to the silent city on the cliffs. Even so, Niño and Chuana were not careless. Each night they drew up the ladder and each day laid it aside in hiding, so that should any persons come innocently that way they would not see it in place, and would not be tempted to climb it and explore the cave, as they had been themselves. Still, there were no intruders and summer only deepened its beauty on Beaver Creek.

The sycamores, black walnuts and velvet ash leafed out with the cottonwoods to cloak the canyon floor in a vivid slash of varied greens. Beneath their taller cover grew the lesser tree-shrubs of the Beaver; the catclaw acacia with its podlike beans, the western soapberry, the false palo verde showing off its flashy yellow dress, the feather-leaved, needle-thorned wait-a-bit, the slim desert willow wearing her gorgeous tiara of pale lavender blooms, the lovely graythorn, the stout mesquite, the netleaf hackberry, the saltbush, the seepwillow, the pungent mimosa and the delightfully fragrant Mormon tea plant. Beneath these, again, ran the riot of fleshy broadleaves, delicate forage grasses and brilliant small groundflowers of the high desert. The sum effect was that of the coolest, most aromatic and colorful oasis imaginable; and, within the haven of its creek-watered depths, Niño and his Aravaipa bride knew eight months of respite from cruelty and fear.

It was in September that the baby came, and that the idyll as ended.

8

"But he is ten days old!" said Niño proudly. "Old enough, very nearly, to ride a pony, much less be carried out on a walk! Come, woman, we will put him in the cradleboard and let him see what the world is like beyond the ladder. Do you feel well enough?"

Chuana had never seen such a change in a person. The child had made Niño a boy again. Since the hour of his birth the little one had scarcely had time to nurse, for Niño's attention. It seemed, indeed, to Chuana, that each passing day of the father's admiration and coddling of the boy erased some new line of the old life from Niño's haunted face. She knew that Indian men doted on their children in the infant age but this devotion of Niño's was exaggerated by his own loneliness. As he loved the mother, so he loved the child—beyond any normal measure.

But Chuana was still weak. She had lost much blood at the birth, was not yet healed. She feared to go out and down the ladder, thinking it would start her to flowing again. It was not in her soft heart, however, to deny the light of excitement in Niño's eyes.

"Well, warrior!" she chided him, "if you can find the strength to place the ladder, I am sure your woman can lace on the cradleboard! Come, why do you sit there? Are you afraid of a little work?"

Niño got up from the breakfast fire in the rear cavern. He went around the firepit to where Chuana sat feeding the boy. "Let me carry him," he said. "Bring the board, but let me carry him for the first part, and to help you down the ladder. All right?"

Chuana smiled, handed him up his son. "It makes me glad, Niño, that you would want to carry him," she said. "Take him and be careful. I will be down presently."

He went out to the ledge cradling the boy as though he were made of willow tissue and would crush at the slightest undue squeeze. When he had gone, Chuana arose with wincing difficulty. She walked with back-muscles bunched, legs moving closely, the strain showing plainly in her dark eyes. She felt better after a moment, and fetched down the cradleboard from its niche and followed Niño outside. He and the boy were already below.

"Easy now, old lady!" laughed Niño, steadying the ancient ladder. "One must take great care at your age; the bones grow brittle and the step unsure."

She smiled again but did not answer, saving her strength. Once on the canyon floor, with the bird song and the chatter of the creek and the warm medicine of the autumn sun invading her limbs, she felt the first real energy since the birth. Its upsurge tempered her fear. Now, when she smiled, the shadow was gone from her eyes, the hesitancy from her voice.

"Where shall we go?" she said to Niño. "Up the stream, or down?"

"I thought you would like to see the horses," answered Niño. "Your mare misses you, and I'm sure little Na-chay would take great delight from meeting the foal. I have been gentling him to stand still with a bag of sand on his back. I made its weight just that of Na-chay. We can let him sit his first pony, I think. Would you like that?"

"Oh, yes!" cried Chuana. "How is poor little Pack-rat?"

They were not talking of the real Packrat. This

"poor little" Packrat was the mare's rusty red foal. They had named him from his small beady eyes, extra large and roman nose, and from his short sturdy legs and oversize girth.

"Why," said Niño, "he is fine, of course. He is like Na-chay, here. All he does is suck on his mother and sleep. He doesn't even have to chase away any flies. The mare stands over him and switches them away with her own tail, I swear it. I have never seen such a mother, excepting for yourself."

"Perhaps," said Chuana, as they started along the creek-side path, "the mare feels as I do; that she will never have another child—I mean, like this one."

Niño glanced at her quickly. She had not meant "like this one." She had only added it after that tiny piece of silence, wherein she had realized her lips had spoken her heart and not her mind. The revelation made Niño uneasy, but he determined it would not spoil the glorious morning ahead for any of them.

"Surely," he said, smiling, "I know what you mean, Chuana. How do you feel now that you are walking your first distance? All right?"

"Yes, all right. Isn't this a lovely day, though? I never heard the birds sing so clearly, or felt the sun so good upon my face. I'm very grateful for it, Niño."

"There's no month like September, Chuana. The whole earth is resting and lying easy. Yes, this is a beautiful day and we are lucky to be alive in it." He paused, and they went along another few paces. Then he nodded and said almost to himself, "I will always remember it, this day and this hour of my life, here, with you, Chuana, and with my son Na-chay."

"Thank you, Niño," she replied softly. "Neither will I forget it—ever."

From above, bellied-down on the scarp of the cliff, the officer studied the Indians through his field glasses. Beside him lay a lean Apache scout, a Tonto, dark-skinned and dry-faced. His eyes, intensely black and glittering, stared at the same scene but with fiercely different intensity.

"Are you sure?" said the middle-aged captain, frowning through the glasses to minimize the heat mirage already wrinkling upward from the canyon floor. "I don't know him, you know. Only from pictures. This damned mirage is bad for so early in the day. We want to be sure. Especially with a woman and child involved."

"It's him," said Lizard. "I would know him ten miles away at twilight. In this morning sun at six hundred yards—" He broke off, nodding his narrow head, low mutter eager with the scent of closing in. "That's Niño, Captain! I told you he was here. Him and the woman."

Captain Orin Milo shook his head. "You didn't tell me about the child," he said. "Damn it, I hate to go after him with that girl and that little baby down there."

"I didn't know about the baby," said Lizard. "When I got that cousin of Packrat's full of *tizwin*, he didn't say anything about any baby; only that Niño and the Aravaipa girl were hiding over in the Verde Valley by the old camp. I remembered this place. We used to come here when I was a little boy. We hunted rock rats in those old Pueblo houses up there by the castle. I told you he might be here, and here he is, just like I said." He clamped his jaw muscles until they moved like snakes beneath his leathered skin. "I'll go tell the Lieutenant," he said, and started to belly back from the scarp edge.

"Hold it!" ordered Milo. "You'll tell the Lieutenant when I say to tell him, you understand, Lagarto?"

Lizard looked at him. "Yes, sir," he said expressionlessly.

Milo raised the glasses again. "That girl," he said presently, "is the one who turned you down, isn't she?"

Lizard's dark face tensed. "What do you mean, Captain?" he asked. "What girl?"

"The one down there with Niño. Chuana. The chief's daughter."

"I don't know what you mean, Captain."

"I think you do, Lagarto. Josh and Nosey told me all about it. You've been after this Niño ever since he left Pash-lau-ta and the others over at Saddle Mountain. But it's the girl you're really after, isn't it?"

Lizard thought a long moment, then nodded. "I knew her before Niño. She would have been mine but for him."

Milo put down the glasses.

"All right, Lagarto," he said, "go back and tell Lieutenant Grimes to go ahead. Tell him to take half the troop and come up the creek from below. I'll take the other half and come down from up above. But remember one thing; you'll be with me. If anything happens to that girl or her child, I'll put a bullet through your back."

Lizard came to a knee, nodded swiftly.

"Would I harm what I have sought for five years?" he said, and slid back from the rim and ran, bent double, back toward the waiting horses of G Troop.

The mare's name was Desert Flower. She was a *grulla*; a smoky mouse-gray, the color of the sandcranes which stood in the shallows of the Gila or the Verde upon one leg and could not be seen a rope-throw away unless they moved. Her foal, Packrat, a pot-bellied, grass-fat little weanling bay didn't need to move to be seen, or rather, heard. His querulous nickering after his dam announced his coming for half a mile in all directions. For the mare's part, she followed Chuana like a pet dog, nosing and bunting at her hand for the tidbit which was there more often than it was not.

Niño had not wanted to turn the animals out. He kept them, during the day, penned in a tiny side-canyon, a little box of rock-walled pasture where they could not be seen either from the rim above or from the canyon floor below and where they had all of shade and water and feed and sunshine and dust to roll in that they might desire, and would stay quiet as well as out of sight because of this good keep. But the mare had pestered Chuana by pawing at the bottom sapling-rail of the cross-fence when they started off without her, and Niño had laughed and said, "All right, let her come," and this was another of those strange things which showed that his life was charmed against his Indian enemies, and that Yosen watched over him where the soldiers were concerned.

They had strolled perhaps a quarter-mile along the stream, away from the corral, when the mare suddenly threw up her head, staring past Chuana, up-canyon. Instantly, Niño froze. From the side of his mouth he said to Chuana, "Do not move except to cover Na-chay's lips with your hand." He gave the baby over to her, as he spoke, and unslung his Winchester. The next moment the mare cleared her nostrils with a soft, pushing snort, and pointed her small ears angling upstream and toward a bend of the current which embraced a long sandspit at the bottom of a cleft in the rim which came down from above. The cleft and the spit were heavy with brush and scrub of a height to hide men, if not horses. Niño knew, too, that the cleft formed an easy decline from the rim over Montezuma's Castle. "The mare smells something," he told Chuana. "Watch her, now, she has cleared her nose. Be ready to go."

"Where?" said Chuana, only her lips moving.

"First, into the hackberry tangle behind us. From there we will have to run for the cave."

"How about Desert Flower? You could make it free on her, Niño. Go, now. You must. Don't wait for them to kill you."

"No, Chuana. If those are soldiers up the stream, there will be others behind us, down the stream. I know how they work. I have led them too many times myself."

"Niño, the mare is winding."

"Yes. Ready, now—"

The desert mustang is like no other breed of horse. It will give its master warning of the enemy, and will watch over him and his camp more keenly, because far more nervous and feral in its recent breeding, than any tamed and faithful dog. Now Desert Flower squatted like a rabbit about to run, and nickered low and urgently in her throat. At once, Niño hipped the Winchester and began to fire. He levered the full magazine into the sandspit brush at the focal point of the mare's staring snort, then dove into the hackberry patch, after Chuana and Na-chay.

By pure luck, his blind fusillade knocked down Milo's sergeant with a raking hit across the collarbone. The man's extreme pain and bursting outcry threw the dozen troopers with Milo flat on their bellies. Their first fire at the Apache couple was thus through the root tangle of their heavy cover, and not as effective as Niño's. More importantly, the moment's confusion gave the hunted Indians start enough to reach the base of the cliff, and to do so ahead of the twenty men down-canyon with Lieutenant Grimes. But it did not give them time to place the ladder before the silent dark-faced Nemesis which had dogged Niño's moccasin prints from the day of the aborted surrender in front of Seiber's tent at San Carlos, caught up with them. Lizard burst from the shadow of the creek foliage and into the bright sunshine of the cliff base, just as Niño seized the ladder from its hiding place.

Chuana, pale as death and sucking with the sound of a wet woodrasp to draw each breath, gasped quickly, *"Look out, Niño! Behind you—!"* and fell, with the warning, and with her body protecting that of Na-chay, among the rubble of rock and cliff-scalings beneath their beloved sun ledge.

As she crumpled, Lizard fired. Niño, hearing the shot blend with Chuana's warning, and seeing her go down in the same moment, assumed the Tonto's shot had felled her. It had not done so, in fact, sheer weakness having caused her to collapse. But Niño was driven past reason, now, and beyond all caution.

He whirled to face the Judas scout.

In his brain was no thought but to kill. In his Winchester there were no more rounds. Lizard did not know this and Niño did not think of it. He dropped the rifle in the rocks at his feet, began going toward the Tonto in a crouching glide—not fast, not slow, but inexorably straight-on. He meant to kill his enemy with his bare hands, and Lizard knew this. He laughed, but it was an unconvincing laugh. Niño merely nodded expressionlessly and came on. Lizard felt his mouth go dry. In his mind many thoughts leaped up in confusion.

This hard devil of a San Carlos was no stranger to him. He had ridden with him. The whites could call him "mad dog" all they wished. Lizard had seen enough of him to know there was always a cold method in his evident rages. But why was he coming at Lizard now? Of what possible importance could Lizard's life be to Niño?

Was it jealousy over Chuana? No, the cursed girl had never looked at any man save Niño. Was it then some idea in Niño's twisted brain that Lizard had cost him his precious sergeant's stripes in the cavalry? Did seeing Lizard scouting for the soldiers, as he had once scouted for them, arouse in him this killing flame?

Again, no. But wait! There was another frightening possibility. Could it be Lizard's foul luck that Niño had heard why it was that he was here with the soldiers? But, bah! How could that be? How could he humanly know that Lizard had been promised amnesty for his part in the Kelvin Grade Massacre, if he could lead the soldiers to Niño? No, no, it could not be. And even if it was, and Niño *had* found out, would he risk his life, and the life of his woman, for a revenge which made no sense at all in the merciless Apache scale of values?

No, and no, and no, reiterated Lizard's racing mind.

Yet, there came Niño, regardless. And at twenty feet a man could no longer trust his mind. Lizard's hand dropped to the holster at his belt. The old-fashioned Colt Dragoon stuck a little in its worn leather. With a curse, Lizard ripped it free. He fired blindly, feeling he could not miss at so close a range; being absolutely sure of hitting his enemy because he had those six shots and there was that so-little space between them.

Many a man, before and since, has died for the same misconception. This was the weakness which Niño knew of. This was the fatal ego of Logarto, the Lizard. The revolver was a white man's gun, and only a very few white men, at that. The Indian never learned to use it right; he never understood its limitations and dangers, never would accept the fact that it was not only possible, but very easy, to miss completely a moving man-target at twenty feet.

Lizard got off the six shots very fast. The cloud of white smoke from the old blackpowder loads was still rolling upward in front of him, when Niño stepped through its acrid wreath and said, sibilantly, "*Zas-tee*, I kill you!"

The Tonto was no coward, and no weakling. He fought well. But the Apache had the great advantage of having walked through his fire, untouched, and the shock of him stepping out of that smoke-cloud and hissing the old Apache killing word, face-close, unnerved Lizard. He was slowed that fraction of a second which allowed Niño to seize his revolver-wrist before he could raise the weapon to strike with it. They went down into the rocks twining and thrashing like two red snakes. From the first instant the heavy long-barreled Colt was the object of combat. Where they fought, the ground was a smoothed rubble of small stones and cliff peelings. There was to hand no rock bigger than a green walnut or a cactus pear. Neither was there any limb, or chunk of iron-hard driftwood large enough to serve as a club. It was *mano-a-mano*, the hand against the hand—until *one hand* might free itself, *and the revolver*, in the same deadly instant.

It was Nino's hand which did this.

By eight o'clock the night was fully down. There was a thin, icy sliver of a new moon gilding the rim above Montezuma's Castle. In the depths below the rim there was only starlight to lessen the gloom of the canyon. On the ledge above the rubble pile where the pueblo of the ancients had slid from the wall, Niño crouched with his son to his breast. He sang a low-voiced Apache prayer to him, a child's prayer which he remembered from his own childhood. The baby slept. Behind them, in the inner room, Chuana slept also. But the baby would awaken and she would not. Niño held Na-chay closer still. He could hear the small heart beating against him. He could feel the delicate breath touch him on the cheek, as the child sighed and stirred. *"Ho shuh, ho shuh,"* he whispered to him, using the Apache gentling and soothing words which he had heard Chuana croon to him, "there is nothing to fear; the night is our friend, Little Na-chay. Soon we shall go. The soldiers will not see us. *Ho shuh, ho shuh,* you will see, my son, you will see—"

Chuana had died as the sun went down. She had lived to see Niño and Na-chay and herself reach the cave shelf in safety. She had lived to load the spare rifle for Niño, as he held off the soldiers trying to come to the cliff's base and get a ladder or a scaling-log up to the ledge. She had lived to see the stark form of Lagarto, twisted upon the rockslide below with his skull and face beaten to a featureless pulp by the steel-and-walnut butt of his own revolver, lie flyblown in the September sun the long day through, until her weary eyes had closed with the last weakness and she had said quietly, "Niño, please take me into our home, that I may see it again while there is time."

He had borne her inside, then, for the soldiers had quit firing, as they always did when it was time to eat, and so he could leave the ledge for the little while that his woman wanted. Thus, as the supper-fires of Captain Milo's command began to sprinkle the twilight along Beaver Creek, below, the spirit-fires in the slowing heart of Eskim-in-zim's daughter flickered and went out in the limestone cavern, above.

No bullet had touched the slender girl. No lack of bravery or determination to live had damaged her. But the soldiers had killed her as surely as though they had placed her dear form against the wall of Montezuma's Castle and driven her down with a hundred times a hundred rifle rounds. Niño did not deceive himself through hatred or dark anger. He had seen the blood coursing from her like a well of black and scarlet water. He had watched her life run out with it, breath by desperate breath, drop by precious drop, smile by frightened, gray-faced smile. And he knew the massive, day-long bleeding had been started by the violent race for the cave from the sandspit ambush on the creek; and he knew that the loss of blood which had drained away his woman's life was not his fault, and not her fault, and not the fault of little Na-chay, who lay now so peacefully against his aching heart. *The soldiers had killed Chuana.* From that hour of that day upon which they had done so, the hand of Niño would be forever against them.

With the thought, the face of the San Carlos youth grew old and ugly as a mummy's. Yet, the following moment, the warm, small body of his son stirred against him and the look softened to a poignant smile. This, in turn, faded swiftly, as he arose and went into the inner room.

There was a crypt in the rear of the cave so skillfully contrived in the manner of its closure that they had lived with it a full month before noting the hand-cut stones which filled its access opening. As careful in their removal of these fitted blocks as had been the old ones in their placing of them, they had seen into the ancient burial niche. It held the skeleton of a small child and they had closed it quickly, not wanting to disturb the spirit of the little one. It was in this limestone vault that Niño now laid to rest his woman. He placed her carefully beside the centuries-dead infant, so that she might know the comfort of its presence, and so that it might feel, too, the nearness of a mother. He put another thing to rest in the niche, as well. A thing which he honored only below Chuana and little Na-chay. It was his sergeant's coat and faded yellow chevrons. So it was that when he had again closed the Pueblo burial chamber and brushed its crevices with rockdust from the floor, making its outlines invisible to searching white eyes, he went forth from the inner room as an Apache—naked but for his leggins, his calf-high *n'deh b'keh*, and the cold steel of his rifle.

He gathered up Na-chay and put him in the cradle-board, strapped to his own back like a squaw. He took no blanket, having used his to wrap Chuana, and hers to wrap the infant by her side. He carried with him six things only: his Winchester, Lizard's revolver, his own canteen, his field glasses, his son upon his back, and, in his sorrowing Indian heart, his vow to avenge his dead love.

He went by the secret cliff trail to the escape cleft, and by the cleft's sloping bottom to the canyon floor. From there it was easy getting to the hidden corral, letting down the gate bars, swinging up on Na-to, "Tobacco," his homely roan gelding, and going through the silent dust of the creek trail, on up the Beaver, and so to the rim, above, via the same exit which had brought Captain Milo's troopers down to the sandspit ambush spot.

When dawn came and Milo's men realized their outlaw prey had left them watching an empty nest, a climbing party was ordered to the cliff. Lieutenant Grimes led this detachment, with Josh and Nosey, sent over from San Carlos to back up Lizard, going ahead to make sure the way was as innocent as it appeared. It was. In the inner room the soldiers saw only what Niño had wanted them to see—nothing. Whatever Josh and Nosey saw, they made no official report of. It was assumed by Grimes that Niño, Chuana and their days-old infant had all used the spidery cliff trail to vanish from the canyon trap, and the matter is so entered in the record to this day.

But young Grimes and his five-man climbing squad were anxious to leave the cave and its empty sun porch. What their hurried eyes could not see, their spirits felt very keenly indeed. There was tragedy in that still, close air, and the growing weight of a thousand years of silence. They talked loud, and some laughed, but they pushed one another to be first back out into the sunshine, and, after that, first down the ladder and back to the noisy, reassuring company of their fellows in the creekside camp. None of them, certainly, stayed on the limestone ledge long enough to see Josh glance back into the cavern and make a sacred sign with his fingers across his breast, nor to see Nosey return the sign, and mutter respectfully in Apache.

"Enthlay-sit-daou, Chuana; abide you here in peace and calmness. . . ."

9

Niño could not keep the baby overlong. He must find a woman for it and he knew but one woman now. Boldly, he struck toward the one place the soldiers would never think to look for him. Following the same trail he had made in coming to Montezuma's Castle, he returned to Kinishba Ruin, circled Fort Apache, crossed over the arid Natanas Plateau and down into the valley of the Gila. It was shortly before dawn of the fourth night, a tremendous single-horse ride *without* such a precious burden as he bore, that he reined-in the roan gelding below Chutanay Mesa, and sent downward toward the sleeping *rancheria* of Packrat the cactus owl signal call.

Packrat was a good sleeper. He was still snoring loudly when his eighty-year-old mother came over to his bed and shook him awake.

"Eh, loafer!" complained the old lady. "I think your friend is up there near the mesa foot. There's been a cursed owl hooting for the last half-hour."

"What!" cried Packrat, reaching for his pants. "A half-hour, and you didn't get me up? I ought to beat you."

"You ought to sleep lighter and eat less," answered the aged squaw. "Besides, am I to get out of my warm blankets on these cold autumn nights every time I hear an owl hoot?"

"I told you of our signal, mother. Damn it, you should have got me up sooner. He may be in bad trouble."

"Bah!" said the old woman. "For Niño there is no other kind of trouble. There won't be for you, either, if you insist on letting him come here every time he's killed another sheriff or shot some more soldiers or done wrong to some new, poor, stupid Indian girl."

"Mother, I've told you he hasn't done these things."

"I know he has."

"Well, maybe that sheriff on Kelvin Grade, or those soldiers at Kinishba Ruin. But that's all. Those lies they tell about him and girls are dirt! As for the sheriff, Niño didn't kill him anyway!"

"How about the soldiers?"

"Yes, he killed them."

"Yes, he did, and you were with him."

"No, I was with the women."

"You were there."

"Yes, all right, mother, I was there. Does that satisfy you?"

The old woman sighed, reaching him his rifle from its antelope-prong rest above the low door. "You were a good boy until you got mixed up with Niño," she said. "Nothing has been the same since then."

Packrat took the rifle. "You mean nothing has been the same since Seiber left, mother. Isn't that it?"

"I suppose. He was a good man."

"Yes, and so was Niño until they drove Seiber away. Seiber could have saved him. They knew that, and they didn't want him saved. So they sent Seiber away."

"Nonsense! you know better than that." The squaw opened the door, peering out into the grayness. "No riders down the valley," she said. "Go on." Packrat nodded, and started out. She took his arm. "Tell Niño that I have some of his favorite tenderloin for him, from that agency beef we got last week. I'll have it broiled by the time you get back." Packrat grinned, patted her white braids. "You try hard, mother," he said, "but it's no good. You always growl at Niño at the same time you're feeding him under the table. Why don't you just admit you love him the same as I do, eh?"

"Hah! that outlaw devil? If it weren't for trying to protect you, I would have turned him over to the Indian Police long ago!"

"Sure," smiled Packrat. "Just like you did Geronimo that time he hid here in Eighty-five. Or Loco in Seventy-nine? Or Benito the year before? Or Chatto the year after? Or Chihuahua that spring the soldiers camped here two days and you had him under your bed the whole while they were chasing him all around the mesa? Oh, yes, dear mother, you're well known for your fierce devotion to the soldiers and the Apache police. Do you want me to send Niño away? Not bring him down here?"

"Go to hell!" said the old lady, spitting out the door before she slammed it shut. "I'll have the meat ready."

Niño licked his fingers, pushed back from the table.

"Mother," he said, "nothing changes, you still broil the finest tenderloin on the San Carlos. Yosen bless you."

"Yosen, eh?" she shot back. "Listen, *bronco,* Yosen has nothing to do with it." She put the baby over her shoulder, patting his back until he belched. "You want to donate some blessings, you better give them to that goat out in the pen. If this baby didn't get some milk right away this morning, maybe you would have had no son tonight."

"He's an Apache, mother; he would have lived."

"Fool! You're the image of all the old ones. You're Geronimo again. Or Chihuahua. Or Natchez. Or Bonita. You think that because you are an Apache that is the whole answer. Well, think about it a little more. Where are Geronimo and Chihuahua and the others? Eh? Tell me that, wild one. But before you do I will tell you that another day on that cooked cornmeal soup and cold water you've been feeding this little *ish-ke-ne* would have him stiff and blue as a stone! Then I suppose you would look at him and say, 'Well, maybe I was wrong; maybe he wasn't an Apache.' Eh? Is that it, outlaw?"

Niño shook his head. "I don't know, mother. Since my woman died I don't seem so sure of many things."

The old squaw's face softened. "Chuana was a fine girl, Niño. But she was never strong. She might have died from the child anyway. Her grandmother did the same thing having her mother, you know; went along for a few days after the bearing, then, *ih*!, like that, she began to bleed again and was gone with sundown."

Again Niño shook his head. "No, mother," he said, "this wasn't the same. The soldiers did this. They killed her. She was all right, doing very well, until they came."

"Niño, that's a lie." The old woman fixed him with her rheumy eyes. "You told me not five minutes ago that she could barely walk when you started out that morning. Be honest with yourself, boy. She could have bled away right here in this *jacal,* lifting a mattress, or hauling wood, or pulling up water from the well. Any small thing could have started the late bleeding. It's a weakness some women have, no different than certain young mares or heifers which will bring you a good foal or calf, then die-up on you and leave you to suckle an orphan. Just like this handful of skin and bones you bring two hundred miles for Old Madre to nurse and hide and save for you. Listen, Niño, I'm telling you this for your own good; those soldiers didn't kill that girl; she didn't die because of them."

Niño looked at her a long time. Finally, he nodded. "Somebody killed her, mother. Who was it?"

"Don't you know, Niño?"

"Lizard? Are you saying the Tonto did it?"

"No, it was not a Tonto."

"Who, then?"

"A San Carlos."

"A San Carlos," he repeated after her, and softly. "That leaves Josh and Nosey."

"And one other," said the old woman.

The truth came hard to Niño. Packrat and the old squaw saw the lines of his face draw in. They saw the look of anguish and pain and remorse twist the dark features, as though to the drive of an arrow through the body. But they saw, also, the look of the *bronco,* of the wild one, which superseded the moment of human weakness, of disarmed sorrow for the loved one, and they knew the time had passed when Niño might be brought to see himself as others saw him, or to hear what they might say to him even in dearest friendship of Apache faith.

"Well, mother," said the outlaw, breaking the quiet of the *jacal* kitchen, "perhaps you are right. Maybe, as you say, it was Niño who killed his own woman. It doesn't matter. Niño still lives and Na-chay still lives, and they are Apaches." He paused, face relaxing, as his dark eyes studied the white-haired figure by the hearth fire. "Now, mother," he said, "you have taken us in and fed us and let us rest here at your own danger. No Apache forgets such a thing in bad times like these. I will forget what you say and remember what you do. And, as to that, there is one more thing I would ask of you and Packrat."

The squaw scowled and fussed with the baby and pretended not to hear him, but finally said, "Well, ask it! Do you think I have all day to sit here waiting?"

"Where is Hoosh?" said Niño flatly.

"Hoosh!" she cried. "That fool girl? That brazen thing who lives alone like an animal out in the brush? That thin nothing which this simple-minded son of mine moons about the entire time? *Ih!* I will tell you not a word of Hoosh!"

Packrat, looking very uncomfortable, made a sign to Niño. The latter nodded and said to the old woman, "Very well, mother, think no more of it. It was only a matter which Chuana wished me to see to. Yosen guard you."

"The hell with Yosen!" the old squaw called after them, and he and Packrat went out the door. "You stay away from that Aravaipa chit, you hear? Both of you. She's no good!"

Packrat closed the door and leaned against it, sighing.

"You see, Niño," he said, "the trouble is that we had Hoosh here for a while, and I could not get her to be my woman. Instead of blaming me for failing as a man, mother blamed Hoosh for being a wild, bad woman. She called her a *bronco,* as she does you. *Ay de mi!* if she only knew the reason Hoosh wouldn't have me—won't have any man—she would have hit you over the head with that tenderloin, just now, instead of broiling it for you! As it is, poor Hoosh gets the reputation for being a loose woman, where the truth is she's still a virgin. I think."

Niño glanced up suspiciously. "What do you mean you 'think'?" he demanded.

"Well, only that—well, you know, Niño—you would know better than I."

Niño's scowl deepened. "Why me?" he said. "Are you trying to say I've been with Hoosh? You're crazy, Packrat. We never even talked in that direction."

"Perhaps not, Niño. But how about looking in it?"

"There were no looks either. I treated her as your woman. I thought you two would marry later on."

"I don't mean your looks. How about hers? She says she looked at you where we stayed on Carrizo Creek, and that you understood what she meant. How about that?"

Niño looked away down the long run of the Gila river, where the morning sun was just turning the banks and waterside foliage a shimmering golden pink. He was thinking back to the cave and to that look of Hoosh's, and he did not try to lie about it.

"Yes," he said, "it's true; she looked at me and I understood her. But I didn't look back at her. She had no right to say I did that!"

"She hasn't said so, *schichobe*," shrugged Packrat. "Nor even hinted it."

"Well, then, what has she said? Or hinted?"

"About you, nothing. About herself, only, that having looked at Niño, how could she look at Packrat, or at any other Apache? I will say, old friend, that you apparently can do more 'not looking' than most of us by staring our eyeballs sunblind. However, I hold no grudge. I'm too old and set in my ways to take on a wildcat like that Hoosh. You can have her, and welcome to the scratches."

"What the devil are you saying now?"

"Just what it sounds like I'm saying; she's your woman and she's waiting for you. Go take her."

Niño shook his head, bewilderedly.

"I don't want that," he said. "I only meant to leave the boy with her. Chuana had me promise I would do that. She thought you and Hoosh would be together;

that you could raise our son with your own. Now, I don't know—"

Packrat didn't know either, but, as always, this lack failed to interfere for long.

"I will tell you what," he said. "After it's dark tonight, I'll take you over there. It's just around the mesa, on that bench where the old spring is. I built her a very nice little wickiup under those four big cottonwoods that stand around the sentinel rock. You remember the place? Sure you do. Well, I thought maybe I'd get asked to stay one of those nights, but I never did. No matter, though, I was glad to help. She's a fine girl."

"She's an Apache," said Niño, and sounded proud.

"Yes, every bit, you bet," agreed Packrat quickly. "Come, you've ridden the whole night. Take my bed in the *jacal*. I'll keep a watch of the valley from out here under the lean-to. When it's good and dark we'll go see Hoosh."

Niño shook his head. "No," he said. "When it's good and dark *I'll* go see Hoosh."

Packrat winced but stood to it manfully. And a little wistfully. "I wish I was you, Niño," he said. "That sure is a fine girl."

The other Apache nodded. "It's only that you're a little too old for her," he said. "She would take you in a minute, if you were my age, Packrat. You know it."

"Perhaps. It's true I'm nearly thirty. How old are you now, Niño? I forget."

"Twenty-two, isn't it? At San Carlos they always told me I was born in Sixty-nine. Seiber said that was about right. Anyway, Hoosh would have you if you were my age."

"It's nice of you to say so. Go in and sleep now."

Niño sat down on the pine bench beneath the lean-to. He looked down the valley again, then at the climbing sun.

"Hot today, for fall weather," he said. "Beautiful month, September. This is the last day of it, I think."

Packrat sat down by his side. Taking out his silk pouch of tobacco and husks, he held the materials out to Niño. The latter helped himself, rolled a husk *cigarillo.* Packrat struck and held the match. He puffed noddingly.

"That's good tobacco. Fresh."

"A week old only. From San Francisco."

"Army tobacco?"

"Yes. I stole it yesterday."

"Have you been caught lately?"

"No."

"Do you see or hear anything of Seiber?"

Packrat was surprised and showed it. "You ask of him?" he said. "I thought you were done with him."

"No, I had time to think much of him this winter over in the canyon. I don't think it was he who fired at us."

"I don't think you ever thought so, Niño. You are just quick to anger, and you are too suspicious all the while."

"Yes, it's the way I stay alive."

"I suppose. I'll give you some of this tobacco to take along. I was going to carry some over to Hoosh anyway."

"That's good. I'll take it. Thanks."

"It's nothing."

They sat smoking. Heat waves began to wrinkle the air over the river flats. Suddenly, Niño began to talk.

"I will tell you what I'm going to do, Packrat," he began. "First, I'll see Hoosh and ask her about the baby. Then I will go down into Sonora and stay with Massai and the Geronimo people and think about a new life for myself. I must not stay here any longer. I would like to see Seiber, but I am afraid now. I think I would get shot before either of us could say hello. So you tell him I no longer think he fired at me up in Fish Creek Canyon. After a while, you tell him about my son. Don't tell any other person. Not even any Apaches. When the boy is old enough to walk and is learning to say words, take him to Seiber. Give him to Seiber and say that Niño wanted his son raised as a soldier and as a son of his great friend, Seiber. He will know what I mean. If I live, and if Yosen sees fit, I will be back to see all of you when times are happier. Until then the boy is not to know that his father was a murderer and outlaw. Only you and Hoosh and your mother will know that Niño's blood is in him. Lizard saw the baby and heard him cry, but Lizard is dead. The other soldiers, the ones with Josh and Nosey, did not see him, and will forget even more quickly. Josh and Nosey knew there was a baby, surely, and they won't forget like the soldiers. But they are Apaches; I don't think they would say anything about the little one."

He sat silently smoking and tasting his *cigarillo* for a while, before asking presently, "What news came on the telegraph about the fight at the cliff?"

"Just that you and Chuana had escaped. There was nothing about the baby that I heard."

"Good. Josh and Nosey said nothing then. They knew I went out alone. If the report says Chuana went with me, then they said nothing even of her."

"It doesn't surprise me. They're good men when they're sober, and friends of yours, too. Of course, if they get to any *tulapai* or *tizwin*, that's different. No bets then."

"Whiskey is a curse, Packrat. That's why I never touch it. It makes children and idiots out of strong men."

"Oh, by all evidence! I don't touch the stuff, either. Not lately anyway. Not since yesterday. It's very bad for you. Terrible."

Niño had to grin. And felt better for the need. He got up from the bench, ground out his smoke in the lean-to dust, took a final look at the sky. "Rain tonight. That's fine. Any tracks will wash out by morning. You agree?"

Packrat sniffed the heavy air, examined the clouds

lying low and long-formed to the north. "Yes, about midnight. Hard. And long. You could ride a shod cavalry horse carrying two cases of ammunition, and leave no trace when that rain has gone by. It will be a duck-drownder, as Seiber used to say."

"A goose-drownder, you mean. That's what he used to say."

"Duck? Goose? What's the difference? It's going to rain like hell. You think Seiber cares what gets drowned?"

"No!" laughed Niño, "not a bit. Packrat, you're a true friend. Now I can sleep."

"Sleep, then."

"I will, thank you. Call me if you see anything."

"Sure. You rest good, now, Niño. Don't worry."

"I won't, old friend. Good morning."

"Good morning," answered Packrat, almost glumly, and turned to stare disheartened down the valley.

It was hell to be short and fat and ugly and nearly thirty years old, famous only for stealing a few cheap supplies from a fly-blown army post, while your best friend was slender and handsome and fierce-looking and undoubtedly, barring only Cochise and the Elder Mangas, the greatest fighting Indian who ever lived.

It was, anyway, if that hero friend was but brief hours from going to see the slim *nah-lin* you loved with all your homely faithful soul.

And you knew, with ten months vengeance, how she was going to receive him when he got there.

Ih! women!

Or, for that matter, men.

10

Packrat did not see Niño again that year. He waited a full day following the night of the outlaw's visit to Hoosh's lonely wickiup, then rode over to see what had happened. The brush hut beneath the cottonwoods by the spring stood empty and still. To Packrat, the second-best trailer in the territories, the story was clear. Niño and Hoosh had been gone since the first night. The wickiup had been cleaned of supplies and bed clothing. Hoosh's little pony and old packmule were gone from the pole corral behind the house. The threatened rain of the night before had not yet come on, and the trail away from the cottonwoods led due south, toward Old Mexico and the Sierra Madre. Packrat unravelled it only far enough to see it was heading for the Pedragosas, for the ancient Apache Road into Sonora. Then the rain began at last and he knew that Niño and Hoosh were not coming back. He sat there in the raw downpour, his heart heavy within him.

It was not Hoosh running away with his best friend, nor was it Niño failing to come by the *rancheria* to pick up the baby boy. It was something else, and Packrat could not, at first, figure out what it was. By the time, however, that the rain had dissolved the final hoofprint, he did know what it was. It was an Indian feeling. A deep sadness and lonesomeness and almost sorrow to see the last great warrior of his people ride away into nowhere with the wild Aravaipa girl who, like himself, had too much of the old *bronco* blood to live at peace at San Carlos, or any other place where the white man said how the living should be. It was like looking at the trail of the last two Apaches on earth. Like watching the history of your people being washed away before your eyes. It was very melancholy, very mysterious, very Indian. And before he turned to leave that place, Packrat made some strong sacred signs in the air. He was not a great believer in Yosen, true. Yet he knew his friends, Hoosh and Niño, would need all the help they could get. If a good word put in by Packrat might bring them any small happiness, *ih!* why not say it?

Feeling better, the fat brave turned for home.

Little was heard of Niño through that winter. His son, under the care of Packrat's mother, grew well and brought the old woman and her bachelor son a great deal of comfort and reward. They were beginning to be quite happy that Niño had left little Na-chay with them, when the agency people got wind of the fact there was a foundling child out at the *rancheria* and word was sent to bring the baby in and give it over to the better care of the government facilities. To Old Madre this meant possible shipment of the infant away from San Carlos. The family word had been given Niño that his son would be guarded and cherished until the agreed age when he was to be taken to Seiber, in secret. Knowing no other way to honor the pact, the ancient squaw bundled up Na-chay and fled with him over the Pinaleño Mountains, toward the Pedragosas and the road to Mexico. In a narrow, bare-rock pass, high in the Pinaleños, a fierce winter storm caught them. Packrat, trailing-up at desperate pace when he discovered their absence from the *jacal,* found them huddled near the summit. He could not pry loose from the sleeted, snow-driven ground the frozen bodies of his mother and Niño's son, and so he covered them as best he could with carried and piled rocks, and then went back to the *rancheria.* When the agency people came he would say nothing. He was accused, even, of having murdered the old woman and the child, to prevent their obeying the order. He was brought before the military court at San Carlos, where the charge was realistically reduced to one of aiding and abetting an escape from the reservation. He was found guilty and discharged from the service as a scout, ordered to stay off the post but on the reservation, upon penalty of being sent to join Geronimo in Florida. The trial included side-charges of having expedited the escape of Niño to Mexico, and of conspiring with the Aravaipa woman, Hoosh, to this end. To all the charges, from first word to last, Packrat said nothing. His mother was dead, his namesake, the son of his best friend, was dead, his job was gone, his reputation ruined, his freedom taken away. There was nothing left to him save the honor of his word, and this he kept. Neither then, nor later, did he betray it.

But his silence could not protect Niño.

In late winter the report of the tragedy reached the Sierra Madre camp of Massai, through other Indians. That such a thing could have happened was beyond Niño's belief. He had to hear it from Packrat himself. Early in May he appeared on the San Carlos reservation. Packrat informed him that it was true, that Old Madre and Little Na-chay had died fleeing the agency people. Niño's grief lasted a full week, during which time he was on top of Chutanay Mesa punishing and purging himself in the Apache way. He took no food and only one canteen of water. He prayed twenty hours a day. He made fires and sprinkled into them the *hoddentin,* the sacred pollen-dust which made clouds of pure white smoke and the strongest spirit medicine of his people. All the while he was on the mesa, Captain Lewis Johnson knew he was there and made no move to arrest him. Johnson was a good man. He liked Niño and respected the ways of his people. He could not have known, and very likely didn't care to know the subject of the outlaw's prayers. He was told only (by Packrat) that "Niño is purging himself on the mesa," and he replied, "Well, we'll let him alone, but when he's through, you see that he leaves at once and without making trouble. I would go up after him, right now, except that I believe it is better to let him go quietly, if he will."

Yes, Johnson was a good man. But his lenience came too late and it was given in a lost cause. When Niño left the mesa, he had been given his reply by Yosen. He informed Packrat of this chilling fact, when the latter met him at the foot of the Chutanay Trail.

The chubby San Carlos had been terribly afraid while his hunted friend prayed on the mesa top. He had been tempted to go in to Captain Johnson and ask him to come arrest Niño for his own good, and the good of his people. Packrat had seen the bad light in the *bronco's* eyes when the news of his son's death was confirmed. He had read the white prayer smoke up on Chutanay, too, and he had known it wasn't good smoke.

Yet, in the last part, he could not betray Niño.

Maybe it wasn't Niño. Niño was a bad Indian now. He had changed down in Mexico. Those damned Chiricahuas of Massai's had poisoned his mind. Packrat could tell that the minute he opened the door of the *jacal* and saw Niño standing there in the windy darkness, and Niño had said, with a face of stone, "Don't ask me in. Don't tell me you are glad to see me. Don't call me your friend. Only answer if it is true that Old Madre and my son froze to death in Pinaleño Pass. Only say to me, yes or not, and do not try to lie to me that *you* were to blame for it, or do not try to say to me that it was *not* the fault of the damned white people. I know what I know."

When he had told Niño what he had to tell him, the wild outlaw of San Carlos had only nodded and turned away into the night and gone up onto Chutanay.

No, probably it wasn't Niño any more. Probably it was still little Hoosh whom Packrat loved and would protect if he could. But Niño or Hoosh, it made no real difference. He could not turn on the one without hurting the other, and so he did not go to see Captain Johnson, but waited instead that seventh night at the foot of the mesa trail for Niño to come down.

And now Niño was coming along that trail, just above, and Packrat could feel his belly tighten and his mouth go dry. He forced the smile with which he rode forward to meet his old friend.

"Well, now, Niño," he began, "you look a great deal better than you did. Come on home with me and we will have a feast to break your fast. I've got some good things for you."

Niño came up to him and looked at him.

"Do you remember what I said to you at your door the other night?" he asked.

"Yes, of course. But surely you don't still mean those things about our friendship, and so forth. *You,* Niño? *You,* turn against *me,* Packrat? Your blood brother?"

"Packrat," said Niño slowly, "I have no friends. No Indian friends, no white friends. From the time I leave this mesa, do not trust me. Tell all you know, whose lives you value, to stay away from Niño. See that word of this reaches Seiber, too. Tell him he must never try to see me again. Make that very certain to him. For I have prayed seven days upon the mountain and Yosen has answered me, telling me what I must do."

"Yes, Niño," agreed Packrat carefully. "And what is it that Yosen has told you that you must do?"

Niño stared at him, still-eyed.

"Kill the white man," he said, and rode on by him into the darkness.

Packrat saw his friend but twice again after the mesa parting. From that May night, in 1892, the name of Niño came to sit with an evil sound, even upon the Apache tongue. And the legend, and the lies, began to grow.

With eight Mexican Apaches, presumably Massai and his renegade Chiricahuas, he is said to have come up out of the Sonoran Sierra Madre, burning through

Southeastern Arizona like a summer whirlwind, strewing disaster and utter fear and unreasoning panic wherever he passed—or wherever they said he passed. It was certain that he was placed at the scene of a dozen murders by witnesses who knew him well and could legally identify him—that is, if hearsay were accepted as legal evidence. It was maintained vigorously that the new raids were entirely devoid of the innocence of the old days, when every theft of a moulty chicken from the farmer's hen coop, or a piece of bedraggled wet wash from the ranchwife's clothesline, was hysterically laid upon Niño's bewildered doorstep. It didn't matter that no army patrol or sheriff's posse could catch him or any of his alleged band in the act—or anywhere near the act. Everybody knew that calvary men and sheriffs had to ride one horse, while the Apaches changed mounts at every new ranch. Nobody expected the devils to let themselves be taken in the chase. Nobody asked for proof of guilt, for none was needed this time. Niño had furnished his own, irrefutable proof—he was no longer arguing nor protesting his innocence, as he had before. Didn't that hang him up with his own nails? You bet it did. Or so they said.

This much is true, certain Indians committed certain depredations upon life and property in Arizona Territory during 1892. If Niño were the prime culprit, or if it were Massai, or again some Apache forgotten long since, it made no real difference; either to the whites or to the other Apaches living by white law. The legend caught fire with the barns and corrals and tiny settler houses set aflame by the marauders, and the name of Niño became a curse upon the land.

The fear of him, exaggerated or real, penetrated to every level of territorial society. There is, fortunately, preserved in writing, and by a hand originally friendly to him a calm statement of the degree of the hysteria reached late that year. It is contained in the annual report of the Acting Agent at San Carlos, to the Commissioner for Indian Affairs, Washington, D.C. Speaking of his former sergeant of Apache Indian Scouts, Captain Lewis Johnson recorded for history that long-ago 1892:

> ". . . While the reservation Indians are generally adverse and hostile to him, really effective aid in efforts to run him down cannot be counted on from any but those in Government employ. Some of the Indians, believing he will not be caught, fear to incur his or the vengeance of those they suspect to be his friends, and this keeps them from acting against him. Others, disposed to act, if they have firearms, are without ammunition; while the great mass, lacking organization, stand in absolute awe of the fellow. To convey an idea of this I will instance that when the last raid occurred I had some agency transportation (ox teams) enroute to Ft. Apache with supplies; the party consisted of three Indians, one of them a policeman, armed, acting as guard. The news he had appeared on the reservation in some way reached these men and they became totally demoralized, abandoned transportation and scattered in different directions. One, a Yuma teamster, came back here—a distance of over fifty miles, another went to Ft. Apache and the third sought refuge at the Agency sawmill with a small detachment of troops . . ."

On the same day of Johnson's statement of Indian hysteria, the Gila County Board of Supervisors confirmed the equal white fears by posting a $500 reward for the "capture of the notorious renegade . . ."

Accompanying this announcement was another document seconding Captain Johnson's opinion, but not his calm appraisal, of the wily *bronco*. Trumpeted the *Arizona Silver Belt,* of Globe, in page one, heavy pica:

> ". . . During the past three years he has been the terror of Southeastern Arizona, and his record of murder and pillage makes one of the blackest pages in the history of Apache warfare. Knowing every trail and waterhole, every mountain pass and fastness between

the northern boundary of the White Mountain Reservation and the Sierra Madre, Mexico, he has been able to elude pursuers.

"The celerity with which he travels renders his capture by the military almost impossible, and, therefore, the most hopeful plan for the apprehension of the notorious renegade is that suggested by our Grand Jury. If the several counties which have suffered from his murderous raids will act upon it, offer liberal rewards for his capture or death anywhere in the Territory, it will stimulate citizens and friendly Indians to redouble their efforts to run down the outlaw.

"Many of the San Carlos Agency Indians are as eager for his capture as are the whites, as he is their mortal enemy, and incited by a large reward they will work hard to get him. They are familiar with his haunts and their Indian cunning gives them a great advantage over the military and civil authorities in the pursuit. . . ."

With such fanning of the blaze, the Territorial Legislature caught fire. A politically astute member of its derelict body introduced a bill raising the amount of silver dollars for the shooting down of the Mad Dog of San Carlos to *five thousand!* The bill was rendered a true one, its author's future assured (governor when the territory went over to statehood), and the fate of its lone subject signed and sealed.

Maybe.

When the news of a $5,000 bounty was broadcast, the scalp-hunters turned out in packs. County sheriffs, U.S. marshals, township deputies, army officers, professional lonehand manhunters, local cowboys, drifters, prospectors, homesteaders, saddlebums, adolescents, other outlaws, housewives, hired hands, even a few gainfully employed, sober citizens loaded up their deer rifles, hogleg Colt Revolvers, derringers, shotguns or whatever, for a shot at the first passing Apache who looked as if he might have had a hard night, or lacked a steady job.

This natural eagerness to be of service in the emergency was not lost upon the peaceful Apache population. Within a fortnight White Mountain and San Carlos mothers were locking their young ones in at sunrise, and pleading with their menfolk to stay out in the brush until nightfall. If your skin was dark, your clothing poor, your stature short, your hair long, and the only pony you owned to ride was of the potbellied mustang persuasion, your life was worth $5,000—until your death established the fact that it was not. No record was kept of the number of innocent Indian men—yes, and Indian women—killed over the hungry riflesights of the bounty hunters sent afield by the "dead or alive" terms of the Legislature's blood money. No white record, that is. But the Indians kept track. And by the end of the year a condition of near-panic existed among them, and the bill had defeated its own purpose.

At the height of the confusion and furor raised by the reward offer, a startling truth became self-evident to the defenders of the territory. They were chasing their own "tales." Niño had disappeared as quietly and completely as a puff of smoke.

For the first few weeks they couldn't believe it. But by the turn of the year all but the most rapacious among them had abandoned the "silver bait" and gone back to their ordinary arts of chasing cows, deserters, gold-dust, drunks, flies, body lice, boredom or bawdy women.

An entire year wore away—1893—and, with it, passed a great deal of the fear and excitement over Niño. He was not even heard of, much less seen, in Arizona during that time and many came to believe that he had died in Mexico. A detailed story to that effect, complete with cause—tuberculosis—was circulated and given wide credence among the hopeful. Another, even more final test of his demise, was in the record.

Al Seiber, never failing in his faith in the San Carlos youth, had gotten word to him in his mountain wilderness retreat in Sonora, that if he would surrender to him, Seiber, at an appointed time and place, he, Seiber would claim the $5,000 reward money and use it all to employ legal defense and guarantee fair trial for him in the United States Courts. Seiber also pointed out the very good chance that such trial held for clearing Niño of all charges against him, and urged him to demonstrate his own good faith and honesty, by appearing at the rendezvous to hold a preliminary talk. Seiber's assurances of this "good treatment" of Niño, in the face of his known crimes, stemmed from the overt backing of the all-powerful Indian Bureau, and a tacit agreement with the Army that it would not push its case against the San Carlos renegade, providing the Civil Government of the Territory would share the onus of the necessary leniency of prosecution during the trial. As to the latter contingency, the big German had talked with several powers in the Legislature and found them not adverse to putting a legal quietus on the Niño matter.

The plan then promised success. Popular sentiment was high against Niño, but was equally high in favor of seeing him "pacified" one way or the other. And the "other" way had been tried fruitlessly for three costly years.

A great deal of interest was aroused in Seiber's effort to meet with the legendary outlaw, and it was given an unfortunate amount of publicity. When, subsequently, Niño failed to appear at the meeting place—after having returned word to Seiber that he would do so—it was generally believed the failure confirmed the fact of his reported death from natural causes.

Seiber would not accept this view, insisting he knew better. The Indian he had used as go-between was absolutely reliable, he said. The messenger had talked in person with Niño and been assured he was in perfect health. More importantly, Niño had said he was weary of running and wanted to talk surrender on honorable terms.

By now, however, Seiber's part in the exchange had

become suspect. It was suggested that for him to appear to be in a position of contact and influence with the outlaw might do a great deal to lead the Army to think of reinstating him in his old job as Chief of Scouts at San Carlos. Nothing could have been closer to the lie, but when the big German refused, upon demand, to reveal the identity of his Indian courier, his hold upon the situation was lost altogether. Further, public concern over Niño, as public concern over anything to do with the community conscience, now fell off in direct ratio to the earnest desire of the "decent folk" to forget their part in the recent, abortive eagerness to cash in his scalp. His name began to be spoken in the past tense, albeit still uneasily, and the sturdy, virtuous citizens of Old Arizona settled gratefully for an "out of sight, out of mind," policy with regard to the deceased, "notorious renegade."

A certain pudgy San Carlos small thief and one-time scout of Third Cavalry could have told them another story. But he did not. When he returned from Sonora and gave his information on the trip to Al Seiber, Packrat went back to his *rancheria* at the sunrise foot of Chutanay Mesa as secretly and silently as he had stolen away from it.

He never spoke of his mission into Mexico, and he saw Niño alive but one more time after that.

He heard of him, though—and soon.

11

When the Spanish *padres* were in the land, they encouraged their Indian subjects to dig gold from an enormously rich deposit in the Santa Catalinas north of Tucson. If this fabled mine had an Hispanic name, it did not survive its dark-robed exploiters. It gained an American name, however, after they had departed for greener parishes.

The Apaches, not caring either to dig gold or go down on their knees, one day decided to drive the good fathers out of Southern Arizona. This they did, and very thoroughly, too. Yet, before they fled, the friars arranged to close their private mint, until such time as they might return with enough cannon to convert their proud doubters. To do this, they first blocked the drift of their diggings with a massive panel of oak and black iron, then undercut and brought down the mountain from above to camouflage both drifthead and ore dump. To accept this accomplishment, of course, requires a good deal of imagination, but the seekers after the yellow metal have never been caught shy of the ability to project endlessly the improbable. For the next one hundred years men of all skin colors, crafts and creeds prowled the Santa Catalinas in search for the legendary "Mine With the Iron Door."

The Americans, arriving last on the scene, were hardly the ones to diminish the prospect of finding an easy fifty million in pure vein ore, or stacked Spanish ingots. The languishing hunt was renewed for the next quarter-century with typical *Yanqui* energy and determination, qualities, by the way, for which the simple natives had a plainer, less rounded phrase—*Gringo* greed.

No matter that their enthusiasm lacked elegance, the newcomers were not to be denied some return on their investment. In 1893 a bearded prospector whose name lies buried with his broken pick, made a strike in the process of looking for the lost "glory hole" of the *padres*.

It was certainly not the *Mine With the Iron Door* which he found, but it was gold, easy-working high-grade ore, and a sizeable rush resulted. By 1894 there was a liberal sprinkling of small diggings around the original Cañada del Oro discovery. One of these was Camp Condon, located fourteen miles from the supply base of Oracle. And in Camp Condon, on a day in February of that year, the waiting cord of circumstance began to close silently about the missing Apache murderer, Niño.

Life for Packrat was very lonely. The Army would not give him work. It would not allow him to come up to the agency, except on beef-issue days. It would not permit him to talk to his old friends among the soldiers, and even forbade his friends among the Apache police to traffic with him other than to see he got right back to his *rancheria* with his quarter of stingy steermeat—and didn't stray far from his mesa home in between issue days—and didn't entertain any outlaw friends on any dark nights—and didn't take on any more message-carrying jobs down into Mexico—and a half dozen other *"didn'ts"* which became most discouraging after the first few months.

Indeed, things got so intolerable along in the spring and early summer of that first year (1893) that he went down to the Gila below his place and dug a little *acequia* from a side channel into a half-acre of bottomland which was his, and put in thirty rows of corn and ten of melons. But he kept forgetting to let the water flow through the *acequia* into the furrows, or forgetting to shut off the flow, and so his first and one attempt at farming was pretty well *damned* if it did and likewise if it didn't. By and by—about August, when his corn was sixteen inches high and everybody else's was six feet—he was seized by a humanitarian impulse and took his mother's goat and his own gelding and turned the pair loose in the cropland. Not even this part of the venture proved successful, the goat taking the colic from the green corn and swelling up like a poisoned dog. Packrat put his knife into her distended belly, as he had seen the post veterinarian do to the cavalry horses to let out the gasses, but he was a little strong with the thrust and killed her dead as a doornail. The agent, coming by just then, accused him of both destroying the cornpatch and murdering the goat. It went particularly hard with Packrat because the agent had become somewhat boastful of his regeneration and had brought out two ambulances full of visiting ladies and gentlemen from the Indian Bureau and the Southern Baptist Church, to see with their own eyes how a murderous Apache and former consort of the notorious Niño could be induced to lead a useful and peaceful life in the pattern of his white guardians and benefactors. As the party came up to the *jacal* in time to greet the host emerging from the goat pen with bloody knife and string of guttural Apache curses, and as the apparition was sufficient to spook the teams drawing the second ambulance into a wild dash down to and into the Gila, the demonstration was a qualified success. Packrat was penalized six issue-days and didn't get into the agency again until late fall. But, by that time, he had made a lot of antelope jerky and had a fresh quarter and saddle of venison hanging in the lean-to, and was not feeling nearly the pain he had upon the occasion of the agent's visit to *Rancheria* Chutanay.

The situation continued to deteriorate, no matter.

When winter came on—early that year, and cold as the devil—he had been reduced to talking to his horse. Indeed, company had become so scarce, and conversation so needed, that he had let Geronimo into the lean-to and knocked a hole from it through the *jacal* wall, so that they could speak in the greater comfort of a good fire and by the more convivial light of a Rochester hand-lamp.

Still, Geronimo's interests were limited. His temperament, as well, was uncertain. There were times when he would not reply to a civil question, or laugh at a good joke, and Packrat became so annoyed with him, at last, that he boarded up the hole in the wall. Robbed by this selfishness of both heat and light, in addition to the privilege of sticking his jug-head into the *jacal* to keep track of what was going on, Geronimo brooded two days, then kicked in the entire side of the house dividing it from the lean-to and became, thereafter, a full partner in the enterprise.

Packrat thought at first to throw him out, but when he did, the wall-eyed gelding squared around and went to work on the *outside* wall, by which token there was simply no choice but to let him back in, or to spend the winter in the open air with him. Given an elemental option, Packrat surrendered conditionally: he would grant the basic term of sharing the *jacal*, providing Geronimo would settle for the lean-to, leaving the main *sala* to his master. No fool, the old horse pondered the compromise. He knew that before an Apache would shoot his horse, he would murder his wife and children. But since Packrat was without kith or kin, there was no certain telling how far he might be pushed before reaching for *besh-e-gar*, his trusty rifle, or, worse yet, just plain *besh*, his rusted knife. Remembering the goat, Geronimo gave in.

Christmas Eve brought a strange trio of wise men bearing gifts to the door of the forlorn *rancheria* of Na-chay-go-tah below Old Chutanay Mesa on Gila River.

The proprietor, adoze by a snapping mesquite and piñon fire, was dreaming of the happier days when it really was a *rancheria* there by the ancient sentinel mesa. He was dreaming of Old Madre and the families of her other two older sons who had lived there in those times. He was hearing again the laughing and high-voiced calling of the nieces and nephews, the scolding of the old mother, the good, throaty, female voices of his brothers' plump squaws, the solid male comfort of the three sons living together with such women to support and care for them. Then the dream was getting a little less happy. The days of change were coming into it. Old Madre was getting into trouble with the agency people, and with the army, for harboring all those fugitive chiefs and warriors of the White Mountain and Chiricahua Apaches, and, as a result, the two brothers were packing their wagons and their mules and their women, and taking the little, bright-eyed boys and girls, and going away from the *rancheria* at Chutanay, to settle at another and safer place; a place where one day the soldiers would *not* come, and where one day the guns would *not* go off, and the children and the women would *not* fall dead or wounded, with the men. Again, the dream grew lonelier. It was down to Old Madre and Packrat living by themselves in the big *jacal,* and listening in vain for the old sounds of joy and good cheer from the empty beehive wickiups of the departed sons and daughters-in-law. Then it was down to darker times, yet; right down to Old Madre and Niño's little Na-chay freezing in Pinaleño Pass, as they fled the agent's order to surrender the boy; right down to the night when Niño himself came knocking at the *jacal* door and stood staring, black as death, at his only friend, Packrat; and right down to the hunted, beaten face of Niño looking across that last fire in Massai's camp, down in the Sierra Madre of Old Mexico, and to his tired, homesick voice saying sadly: *"Yes, tell Seiber I will come; tell him that I want to come back and be where I was born, to live with my own people, at San Carlos, where I was happy. Tell him I am glad to meet with him where he says, and that I am grateful. Tell him I called him schichobe; that I want to give him my hand again, and to let him help me explain my bad life and maybe be forgiven, as he says. Tell him Niño is his friend, from this fire where we talk, to the end of his life. And tell him, too, that in his heart, Niño was always his friend, and that he has been very lonely and sad to be away from him this long, bitter time. . . ."*

It was as these words of Apache regret etched themselves before his fitful memory, that the sound of Geronimo neighing sharply awoke Packrat.

Leaving his fireside chair, he blew out the lamp and

leaped to the door where his rifle hung in its antelope-horn rest. As he threw the lever to chamber the first shell, he heard the ponies stomp outside and a familiar Apache voice call out in mock threat, "Don't shoot, you're surrounded!" Then a second Indian growling, "Yes, don't be a fool, Fat One, we've got you outnumbered three-to-one! Open the door and throw out your rifle; it's the police—!"

Packrat scowled puzzledly, at the same time his heart warmed to hear those dear good voices again.

"I know very well who it is, you rascals!" he called back gruffly. "And Yosen bless both of you for coming. But you said 'three-to-one,' and these are risky times for me. Let your friend speak up that I may hear him too."

"Ih!" cried Josh, "he's no friend of ours, he's a friend of yours. We've only done you the favor of bringing him out here. Him and two bottles of *tulapai* and a canteen half full of *tizwin*. Come on, open up!"

"Yes, do that," agreed Nosey emphatically, "or we will shoot out your windows."

Packrat hesitated a moment, but only to get his pants pulled up from his ankles, and buttoned.

"Since I know from the windy quality of the talk, where that other half-canteen of *tizwin* is," he said, "and since it's Christmas Eve and I'm lonely enough to let even you two vultures in, and, moreover, since window glass costs like hell and takes two months to get here from San Diego, I'll do as you say. But that *friend of mine* you've brought along better not be a stranger, or a San Carlos spy. If he is, I'll break both your bottles of *tulapai*. That's before I shoot your ponies. Which will be after I've knocked your skulls in. *Comprenden?*"

"Cuidado, amigo," pleaded Josh. "Shoot the horses, knock out the brains, whatever you say. But please don't break the *tulapai* bottles!"

"All right," agreed Packrat, "Merry Christmas—"

He stood back, swinging the door wide and waiting

for the three dusky Magi from Camp San Carlos to stomp in and slap the snow off their coat collars. It was then his small eyes grew large. The third of the faithful was not from San Carlos, nor of Apache complexion. He was so big he blocked out the doorway when he squeezed grinningly through it. He was pink-cheeked as a baby, yet powerful as a boar grizzly. He still walked with a left-footed limp from where Lizard had shot him through the instep four years ago, and he was still the best friend the Apache ever had in Arizona. All Packrat could do was stand there wringing that great bear's paw of a hand and saying over and over again, "Seiber! Seiber, *schichobe!* Yosen bless this house!"

It was a wonderful party.

Seiber was no devotee of *tulapai* but made an exception of the occasion. Packrat, as he had told Niño, was a man who could resist all manner of drink. Unless it was Christmas or he was thirsty. Or perhaps lonesome.

Along about the third round that fine time arrived where tongues and memories had been mellowed, but not yet begun to thicken or grow bitter. The talk, naturally, turned to the old days at San Carlos. Then, to the not-so-old days, and to the mysterious disappearance of Niño.

"Do you suppose," said Josh, "that he really is dead? That he died down there of the lung fever, as they say up at Globe?"

"Of course not!" answered his friend Nosey. "You don't kill a man like that with a little consumption. I've heard that Chuana had it, but I don't believe Niño caught it from her. Still, who knows?"

"Well, I know!" claimed Packrat, smacking his fist into his palm. "You're forgetting that I talked to him *after* he was supposed to be dead and buried of that bad cough. What I came back and told Seiber was the truth. I sat across from Niño as close as I'm sitting from you. He's alive, all right. He's unhappy, but he's not sick."

"How about Hoosh?" asked Nosey. "I always had half an eye for that little Aravaipa myself. No offense, Packrat. We know how you felt about her."

"I didn't see Hoosh," answered the pudgy host. "Niño kept her away for some reason. He did tell me she was well, and that they had a child on the way. Let's see, he said six months, then. It's been six more since. So I guess the little one would be about three months old."

"Why do you suppose he hid Hoosh from you?" Josh put the question, tipping down the last of the first bottle, as he did. "That doesn't seem to make much sense. You think he was jealous of you?"

"Never, you fool. Hoosh had eyes only for him."

"Well, what then?"

"Chin-da-see-lee," said Packrat soberly. "I am sure of it."

"Hoosh, homesick?" Nosey took the empty bottle from Josh, sucked the last drops from its bottom, licked the rim of its neck. "Well, maybe so. Those Aravaipas are a close lot. Especially that Eskim-in-zim blood."

"Yes," said Packrat, "remember she is still only a little girl. What I think happened is that the idea of being Niño's woman has worn a little thin living down there in the Sierra Madre with Massai and those damned Chiricahuas. I will tell you those people are no good. They give me the chills just to have them watching me. Massai most of all. Now, there's a murderer, if the whites want one. Why do they pick on poor Niño?"

Here, Al Seiber nodded, and entered in.

"They pick on him," he said, "because they don't like what he makes them think about, and that's themselves."

"How's that?" asked Josh, uncorking the second bottle with his teeth. "I missed something there."

"No you didn't, Josh. It's just that it takes a white

man to understand a white man, just the same as it takes an Apache to make sense out of another Apache. You see, it's this way: the agency people had a chance to make something out of Niño; they had him since he was a toddler, and they blew their shot with him. Now, Massai, he's a bad Indian. They never had a possibility of raising him the white way, like they did Niño. Massai was a *bronco* to begin with and wouldn't stand for a bridle at no time. Niño, though, he was the best boy, white or red, I ever dealt with. His record with me and the Army up till the damned county grabbed him on that stupid business of doing-in that whiskey peddler, was A-1 perfect. The whites around here know damned well they done wrong by Niño, and they ain't about to admit it. They been trying to kill him ever since they found out they couldn't put him in prison. One way or the other, they mean to sweep him under the rug, and they ain't meant to do another thing by him from the start."

The three Apaches looked at Al Seiber.

Drunk or sober, they had never heard the big German string so many words together at one time.

"Seiber, *schichobe,*" announced Packrat finally, "I'm not sure, but I think you said a lot, just then. Let's have a drink."

Seiber nodded again.

"All right," he said, "pass the bottle."

They all had a gulp, then Nosey, last in the line, set the *tulapai* on the table.

"I've been thinking about your words, just now, Seiber," he said. "It occurs to me that we have a better way of saying the same thing; shorter, anyway."

"You Indians usually manage to get the most across in the least space," acknowledged Seiber. "Have at it in Apache."

Nosey's dark face settled into a scowl.

"What a dog can't eat, he buries," he said. *"And if it's too big to bury, he lifts his leg on it."* His scowl deepened. The *tulapai* and the good company and the

warm cheer of Packrat's kitchen were for the moment forgotten. "I think that's what they've done to Niño," he said. "They couldn't catch him and they couldn't prove he did all those things they said he did, and so they have done the last thing a dog would do—they have urinated upon his reputation, so that no one will touch him—they could not break him to their ways, so they poisoned him. Now even his own people are afraid to come near him. He's as dead as a strychnined wolf."

Josh and Packrat looked at one another.

"Well, you haven't saved any words over Seiber's," said the latter, "but you are right, I think. We'd better have another drink."

"Yes," said Josh, reaching for the bottle. "This could turn into a bad medicine meeting, if we're not careful. Old Niño is safe in Mexico, it's cold as hell outside up here, we've still got nearly a full bottle left and we are wasting good time. Merry Christmas—"

He lifted the *tulapai* to his lips, then passed it on. All drank quickly and a little awkwardly. But the volatile fumes of the corn-mash liquor and the white fire of its race into the belly and through the body soon dissipated all uncertainty and hesitation. The three Apaches led off with a Thankful Dance to the God of Corn, Seiber followed with a rousing baritone rendition of "Tenting Tonight," and "The Battle Hymn of the Republic," Packrat recited the Lord's Prayer, in Apache and while hanging by his heels from the antelope-prong gunrack over the door, and all four celebrants wound up with a footrace, stripped naked, down to the banks of the Gila for a midnight dip in the main channel.

Packrat hit his head on a rock on the first dive and by the time his comrades missed him, he was pretty well waterlogged. They got him back up to the *jacal* and emptied him out but he was still stiff and blue, so Seiber ordered a half-cup of horse linament poured down him. This brought him around and, since it appeared to have no harmful side-effects of its own, Josh and Nosey proceeded to treat themselves to the same regimen, pleading that it was pure blind luck which had brought Packrat to find that rock in the darkness, and that it was only fair they should be provided equal protection. When Seiber inquired as to protection from what, they answered that they were going back down for another swim, and might hit a rock themselves. At this point the big German figured things had gone about far enough for a white man, and retired for the night into the safety of the lean-to. It was somewhat aromatic in there but it was by no means the first time he had bunked with a horse. Despite Geronimo's snoring and authoritative fragrance, he was as warm as a bearskin rug full of hot water bottles, and Seiber slept like a child until the sun was five hours high and Geronimo accidentally stepped on him while trying to nuzzle his tobacco pouch out of his back-pocket. By that time, Josh and Nosey had long since gone and Packrat was getting breakfast. Seiber sat up, grabbed his tobacco pouch away from his mustang bedmate, groped his way into the kitchen alcove, inquired plaintively of Packrat:

"Good morning, *schichobe;* where the hell are we—?"

Seiber stayed the day. He left the following morning, saying he had business at San Carlos, then must get back to his work over by Tucson. Packrat politely refrained from inquiring into his aims at the agency, but did inquire as to what he was doing in the Tucson area. "Do not tell me," he said, "that you are still thinking to get rich like those other fools over there, eh? No, I won't believe it of you again. Not after what you said about your waste of time up in Fish Creek Canyon. You've found a good job, that's it. What are you doing, driving the Tucson stage?"

The white man grinned sheepishly. "You know what I'm doing," he replied, tightening his cinch and advising his horse to stand still on pain of getting its ribs kneed-in. "It's true we didn't get enough out of that

Fish Creek strike to buy the beans. But you know how it is with gold."

"Sure I do. You white people are crazy. I thought you were different, but you're still digging in the ground for what's not there. How did the whites get so strong, being so stupid?"

"Being stupid is no handicap," laughed Seiber, testing the snugness of his saddle. "It's when a man gets smart that he's heading for trouble." He swung up, held down his hand. "Well, *schichobe,* it's good-bye again."

Packrat shook his hand, wrung it quickly.

"Yes, it seems that everything moves too fast these days. There isn't even time to talk any more. There are many things I wanted to ask you."

Seiber bobbed his head. "Tell you what," he suggested. "Why don't you saddle-up and ride back with me? I think I can get the agent to give you a ten-day pass. What do you say?"

Packrat looked at the gray sky, hunched his back. "Too damn cold," he answered. "You go ahead."

"No," insisted the big German, "I mean it. I've got a nice little shanty over there in the hills. Plenty room for the both of us, and I'd like to get some talking done, too. I still think we might be able to get in touch with Niño again. He tore his shirt with the voting citizens when he didn't show up for that final meet with me, but I didn't read it that way. The poor devil just lost his nerve at the last minute, I figure, and I got a hunch he'd come in given another, not so noisy, chance. It's why I come over here to San Carlos. Wanted to talk to Captain Johnson about it."

"Yes? What did he say?"

"Said he'd think it over. Said meanwhile why didn't I try to get in touch with him if I could."

"And you think you can?"

"With your help."

Packrat thought about it. Finally, he hunched his back again, teeth chattering to the morning chill. "No," he said, "I'm afraid of him now. I think he's been driven too long. His mind may be gone. He acted peculiar when I was down there. Made me feel uneasy."

"Naw, that's not so! You were spooked by that devil Massai. And I don't blame you. But you can't tell me Niño has gone off his rocker. Not him."

"You didn't see him."

"True." Seiber swung his horse. "Well, Packrat, you think about it," he said. "If you hear anything you think I ought to know, you send word right away. All right?"

"Sure, all right. Where did you say your mine was?"

"In the Catalinas, north of Tucson, up near Oracle. Place called Two Squaws."

"You got any friends with you, this time? If so, maybe we'd better change the signal call. Last time all I got for my owl hoot was a rifle bullet fired out the window."

Seiber's pleasant face hardened.

"Yeah," he said, "those damned fools. I always felt they was responsible for everything Niño done after that."

"*That* damned fool," corrected Packrat quietly. "There was only one gun firing. Niño and I know whose it was."

"Yeah," said Seiber again, "you and everybody else in Arizona. He's sure advertised it enough since."

"Maybe *too* much," nodded Packrat grimly. "You know Niño."

Seiber eyed him. "You think he'd try it?" he asked.

Packrat shrugged, answered matter-of-factly. "What would you do," he said, "if Wallapai Clark had poisoned your life with his lies?"

Seiber frowned. "I don't like to think," he said. Then, squinting at Packrat, "You still believe Niño about that William Diehl killing, don't you?"

"I believe what Niño told me. Why would he lie to me?"

"No reason, I guess. It's the same old story, though; who do you believe, Niño or Wallapai Clark."

"No!" Packrat was quick with it. "The real story goes this way: Who do you believe, a dirty murdering Apache or an honest God-fearing white man?"

The big German studied him. "You've memorized them words pretty bitter," he said, "but I don't blame you none. When it comes down to choosing between Niño and Wallapai, I made my own pick same as you. I ain't seen Wallapai since Fish Creek." He shook his head, frowning again. "Funny thing, though," he added, "I heard of him just before I rode over here. Him and John Scanlon both. They got a claim in the next camp over the ridge from mine, it seems."

His companion's beady eyes narrowed. "*Anh,*" he said, "is that so? Tell me the name of that camp. In case I ride over to see you, I'll want to give it a wide circle."

"Condon," replied Seiber, "Camp Condon." Then, waving with a final smile, "*Adios, amigo.* I'll be looking for you when the weather turns."

"*Adios, Jefe,*" said Packrat, returning the wave with the old Apache Scout salute. "Ride with Yosen."

He went back into the house, then, and back to the business of being lonely. There were no more visitors to the Chutanay *rancheria* that year and Packrat thought no more of his parting words with Seiber until a certain day in the second month of the New Year. On that day, again a bad one, windy and cold, he returned from a deer hunt over by the Big Rock spring behind the mesa about dusk. By the time he got Geronimo stabled—they had had a misunderstanding and the mustang was back in his pole-corral next to the goat shed—it was full dark, with the wind coming on once more to howl like a pack of wolves.

There was some trouble getting the *jacal* door open and Packrat, tired by the hunt and depressed at having seen Hoosh's little abandoned wickiup at the spring, began to kick and curse at it. He was astonished to hear a giggle within the shelter, followed by the scrape of the drop-bar being withdrawn from the inside, and some reprimanding, happy words in a voice he had feared never to hear again.

"Please! please!" cried the trespasser, *"there is a lady present!"* and with the reproof, Hoosh swung the door open and threw her arms about Packrat's neck and began to cry as though her heart had burst.

When her emotion had subsided, and when Packrat's own heart had quit beating with the wild excitement of seeing her again, they got the door shut, the lamp lighted and the piñon coals blown to life in the flagstone fireplace. Hoosh kept chattering three miles a minute, after her customary way, and Packrat just sat and let her talk, his eyes and his heart feasting on her dear form and luminous, great-eyed face. She worked as she talked, though, and she was a real woman, not a wispy one like Chuana. Before Packrat realized it, she had built up the fire with mesquite chunks, had the left tenderloin peeled out of his spikehorn buck and broiling over the pungent flames, and the coffee pot singing on its black-iron hook. He didn't recover himself until she had brought him his *jacal* moccasins, helped him out of his hunting shirt, put him down in the cowhide chair by the fire and seated herself at his feet on the old bear robe of the hearth.

Then he began to hear what she was saying; to start listening and stop looking.

". . . and so, little Packrat, dear friend," she was beaming up at him, "at last Niño has done what you wanted him to do. He has come up to see Seiber and he has promised that this time there will be no turning back. Even as we sit here and smile with our gladness to see one another, he is riding through the night, going to Seiber. Isn't it wonderful, Packrat? We're home again. We can all be together once more. You can take the baby on your knee and you can love her just like the other one, for I named her after you—Nachita—even though she is a girl. Oh, Packrat, wait until you see her! And wait until Niño gets back from seeing Seiber over in the Catalinas. We will all have such wonderful times again!"

Watching her face glow, hearing her voice thrill, Packrat felt a cold shadow fall over him. He could not say why he shivered when he should have been laughing with his dear Hoosh, who was so happy. But there was a dark warning of some kind hidden in her last words, and he spoke to her very carefully.

"Where have you left the baby, Hoosh?" he said. "Over at your grandmother's on Aravaipa Creek?"

"Yes, oh yes!" she said, eyes shining. "We'll ride over there as soon as Niño gets back. He told me to come up here and wait with you, in case there was any trouble. Also to let you know we are here, and that he knows, now, that you and Seiber were right. Aren't you glad. Packrat!"

"Hoosh," he said gently, the cold growing in him, "how did Niño know where to find Seiber?"

"Why? Massai told him, I think. Some of the Chiricahuas heard it from their relatives at White Mountain Reservation. They said the news was that Niño's old friend was digging for gold again, and had told the Apaches he met that he wanted to see Niño once more, and told them where he was, over in the Catalinas."

"*Where* over in the Catalinas?" said Packrat.

"Oh, one of their gold camps close to Oracle."

"Which one, Hoosh?"

"Why, I don't remember right at the minute, Packrat. Does it matter? Do you think it makes any difference?"

"It makes a very great deal of difference, do you understand that, Hoosh? Think carefully now—was it Two Squaws? Was that the name?"

The girl shook her head. "No, that wasn't it. It was a man's name, an American. It had nothing to do with any squaws. It better not have, anyway!" she laughed.

"Hoosh," said Packrat, "was it 'Camp Condon' where those Chiricahuas told Niño to seek Seiber?"

"Of course! That's it! *Camp Condon.* Isn't that wonderful, Packrat? I remembered—!"

Packrat didn't answer her.

He was already on his way to the antelope-horn gunrack over the doorway.

12

Wallapai Clark came out of the cabin and looked at the weather. For February, it was a nice day, he decided. He and Scanlon might as well get into Oracle and fetch those supplies. Matter of fact, they might as well go down to Tucson and get them. Wouldn't take much longer and they could have exactly what they wanted that way.

"Scanlon," he called into the claim shack, "she's going to turn off nice. We'd best saddle-up and take out."

His partner came out, checked the sky. "Some dark stuff to the northeast," he observed, "but I allow you're right; we'd ought to be able to make it back in time. You want to take the mare or the mule?"

Clark was not a big man. Lean and spare, he had a temper to go with his lack of height.

"Damn it to hell!" he snapped, "why for you have to ask such idiot questions all the time? You know the mare's shy a shoe. You think the Good Fairy come down and bent one on for her last night?"

"Well, all right, so we'll take the mule. You don't need to bite a man's head off about it."

They were an odd pair, Scanlon as big and quiet and under control—dumb, Clark called him—as his partner was quick and acrid. But they got along because their luck had been good together. They didn't like one another but neither would leave the other for fear he might leave the "luck of the camp" with him. Of the team, Clark was the brains, Scanlon the brawn. Between the two talents, they had found and dug a lot of ore, and so they kept at the partnership, watching that things didn't wear too thin.

"Sure, sure," said Clark, grinning tightly. "Forget it. I couldn't sleep last night. It spoilt my breakfast."

Scanlon let it go. "I'll get the mule," he said.

"All right." Clark picked up his Winchester from beside the door. "I'll go down the gulch and ask Mercer to keep an eye on the place while we're gone. You never can tell."

Scanlon scratched his head. "Tell what?" he asked. "We ain't got a thing nobody would want. Why pay that Limey kid a whole dollar to watch nothing?"

"You call that mare nothing?" Clark barked at him.

"Well, my God, who'd want *her,* Wallapai? Wouldn't nobody but a damned 'Pache have the gall to be see'd with her in the broad daylight. She ain't worth the work to cut her up for wolf bait. Sometimes I do believe you have got the worries worse nor a old woman—Jesus!" he broke off suddenly, "you *are* fretting about the 'Paches again!"

For reasons of his own, Clark hated to be reminded of his preoccupation. He had been one of the best scouts for the Army in his day, and his Wallapai Indians had been among the best of the native trackers employed to run down the outlaw Apaches. Yet, clearly, he had never taken the red man, Wallapai or Apache, at their own valuation of themselves, as say, had Seiber, Tom Horn, and some others. If the latter were to be called first "professional scouts" and then "white men," Clark would have to be called secondly a "scout" and primarily a "professional white man." A fearless man who did not hesitate to serve the territory when many other of its citizens only looked, or indeed, ran the other way, he was none the less and on his record, an avid Apache hunter. If the words rabid and hater were substituted for those of avid and hunter, the statement might be still closer to the truth of Edward A. "Wallapai" Clark's feelings toward the children of Cochise and Mangas Coloradas.

In either case Scanlon's present barb struck an old, unhealed wound, and Clark wheeled upon him.

"You're right I'm fretting about them!" he cried. "As long as there's one of the devils running loose in Arizona a white man's life and property won't be safe. If I had my say the whole lot of them would be rounded up and shipped down there to Florida with Geronimo. And I mean every dirty-blanket squaw and squealing kid among them, too; I ain't just talking about the *bronco* bucks!"

Scanlon bobbed his head soberly. "It's small wonder you can't sleep, with all them charitable notions bottled-up inside you," he said. "Seems like you'd just naturally blow up and bust one of these here nights."

The burly Irishman was not given to irony and Clark didn't know what to make of his remark, but took no chances of overlooking it. "Save your funnybone for the mule!" he glared, before stomping off down the creek, "he's more your speed!"

Scanlon stood watching him until he was out of earshot, then jutted his big jaw defiantly, if carefully.

"Well, anyways," he said, "me and the mule sleeps nights—"

The man was white, and dirty, and dangerous-looking.

He came over the ridge behind the claim of Wallapai Clark and John Scanlon, skulking like a prowling wolf, which, essentially, he was. Three weeks escaped and on the run from Yuma Prison, he was starving to death and desperate for two things; a mount and a bait of grub to go over its withers. Below him, he saw the old packmare and the neat, well-kept cabin. He saw, too, the empty look of the place, a look which is quickly learned by any hunted man, and he knew that luck had dealt him a hand at last.

Two days before, he had murdered an aged Papago Indian in Sabino Canyon coming out of Tucson. He had wanted the old man's clothes and his horse, and had not wanted to take them leaving any witness. But the horse had fallen on the slick rock climbing over the pass into the Canyon Creek drainage, and broken a shoulder. He had cut its throat and was about to butcher it, when four cowboys had come along and nearly caught him. They had fired on him in his Indian rags, and run him five miles up the mountain before turning back. He had not dared return to the dead horse, and had made his way on foot down the other side of the divide into the Cañada del Oro diggings.

Drifting along the creek he had scouted each camp for the supplies he must have. The Clark & Scanlon claim was simply the first one he had struck which gave promise of "nobody home."

Yet, now, as he started out of the brush, he saw the young man bathing in the creek below the cabin. He did not hesitate this time. Not even to take steady aim. He fired cursingly, and was amazed to see the miner jump out of the water and run for cover, unharmed. The next moment he was cursing again, for his fire was being returned from across the creek, and he realized the young fellow had had his clothes and rifle in the farside rocks.

Now he had to move with no more misses.

Getting and keeping the cabin between himself and his hidden victim—now turned assailant—he slid from his own cover and got to the horse-pen behind the shack, unseen. There was only a halter and a packsaddle for the old mare but he took these gladly. Another five minutes sufficed to ransack the cabin for some leavings of flour, beans, sugar, coffee and a moldy piece of side-meat. All went into a feed sack slung over the pack-saddle. The mare ready, he slipped to the down-gulch corner of the cabin. Listening, he heard voices approaching from some of the lower diggings. He had thought the shooting would draw the other miners up the canyon, but he did not let this threat disconcert him. Firing another three rounds at the cross-creek position of the bather, he seized the mare's lead-rope and scrambled with her back up into the brush from which he had emerged not ten minutes before. He was over the ridge, out of sight and hearing by a safe quarter-hour, when the first of the downcreek miners puffed up the slope to the Clark & Scanlon cabin.

With the young Englishman, Mercer, they went over the ground out back, examining both corral and cabin areas for footprints. All they found were the tracks of some worn-thin Indian moccasins, but the verdict, *semper idem,* was rendered on the spot.

"*'Paches—!*" announced "Cochise" Jones, a bearded elder who had served with Crook, and all the assembled heads bobbed dutifully and that was that. Shots had been fired at a white man. A horse was missing. A cabin rifled. Moccasin prints left behind. It made no difference that no one had seen an Apache, or that half the white scouts and hunters in the territory wore Indian footgear. There was no fun in being attacked by whites. Indians, now, that was something else again.

Especially Apaches.

"I don't know," said Packrat, scanning the country ahead, "I just don't know. I hate to let you do it, but I think I'll have to."

Hoosh smiled. "Why worry about me?" she asked. "I can find Niño all right. If that's the trail down there all I need do is wait along it until he comes by. He surely can't have beaten us over the mountain. Not on that old broodmare he borrowed from Grandmother."

Packrat scowled, continuing to study the problem.

They were in a saddle, above the headwaters of Canyon Creek, and above the mining camps farther down in Cañada del Oro. The odds were large that they had, indeed, come to this place ahead of Niño. For some reason he had given Hoosh his good horse, Tobacco, and with Packrat's own Geronimo, he and his slim companion had made fast time from Chutanay Mesa. Since Niño had but an hour or two start on them, one had to accept Hoosh's confidence on the matter of intercepting Niño on his way into Camp Condon. But, then, Packrat had taken a shortcut which not even Niño knew of, and therein lay the danger of the matter. He wished, now, that he had followed his first thought to ride the regular Tucson Apache road through the Catalinas, as no doubt Niño had done, in this way coming up to his old friend on the trail. But that course had had two prime dangers. The first was that it was not safe for anyone to come up behind Niño, and the second was that if Niño should travel faster than they, doing so by stealing horses along the way, then they would not head him short of Camp Condon and the whole thing would be wasted, and not just for Niño. Should the outlawed San Carlos be jumped by the miners in the Cañada, the entire countryside would be up in arms and on the lookout for *any* Apaches. He and Hoosh would get no better reception than Niño, under such circumstances. But, then, damn it, somebody had to get to Two Squaws and bring Seiber fast. With the big German in Camp Condon to look out for Niño's safety, they might all come to a happy conclusion. But if Niño were *seen* before Seiber could be brought over the ridge, then Yosen help the three of them.

No, it was not a simple decision Packrat faced sitting his wall-eyed pony up here in that high saddle above Canyon Creek and Cañada del Oro.

Yet it must be made.

"Hoosh," he said at last, "we will do as you say. You go down there at the creek fork and wait for him where the main trail comes in from San Carlos. Hide in those alders and little pines. That's your only cover. Keep your horse quiet. Wrap your reins around his muzzle if any riders come by on the Apache Road. I don't think they will."

"Neither do I," shrugged Hoosh, "but in any event don't worry about me. What do you think I have learned from all these months with Niño in Mexico, nothing at all? I'm a better scout than most men now."

"I believe it," said Packrat admiringly. "You wore me out coming over the mountain. You didn't make one mistake either. You learned pretty good, all right."

"From you," the slim girl laughed, "I will accept such flattery. Niño always said you were the only Apache who might ever catch him."

"He said *Apache,* eh?"

"Yes. Why do you ask?"

"He said it on purpose that way. He meant there was one white man who might do it too. And he's right."

"Seiber?"

"Yes."

"*Ih!* I don't believe it!"

"You think you know more than Niño?"

"Pah! he didn't say anything about Seiber!"

"Take my word for it, Hoosh, he meant him."

Hoosh's blood was up now. Niño had diminished no fraction to her bright eyes in all the hardship and danger he had brought to her since Chuana's death. No man lived, white or red or brown, fit to hold his horse at a waterhole, let alone be ranked his equal, or possible superior, in any skill of the war trail. She turned now to prove it.

"Nonsense, Packrat, don't make me angry. If Seiber was able to find Niño he would have done so. How do you answer that? Why hasn't he come and caught him long ago? Don't try to lie to me; just admit you're wrong!"

Packrat pursed his lips. "You're an Aravaipa, so maybe you never heard it," he said. "But we San Carlos have a saying: 'Never argue with a packmule or a pretty girl.' "

"Hah! so you admit it!"

"Yes, sure. Come on, now, are you ready to go? The way is clear, so you better hurry. Remember, you and Niño will meet Seiber and me up here, not down there." He pointed to the creek trail below, and she nodded.

"Yes, I remember. Good-bye, dear little Packrat."

"Good-bye, Hoosh."

She started off, then held back. "Is there any particular time to tell Niño to expect you?" she asked.

He nodded quickly. "Tomorrow sunset."

"That's a long time for such a short ride." She was frowning slightly, shaking her small head. "It isn't even sunset today yet."

Packrat sighed heavily. "Whenever an Apache rides these days, it's a long time," he said. "The trouble is to find one white man without finding any others. That takes a lot of sniffing and circling."

"Yes, of course." The tiny girl's bright smile flashed again. "Well, *cuidado, hombre,* here goes Hoosh—!"

"Cuidado, Chiquita," he called after her. Then, under his breath and with a sad-faced, hopeless wave:

"Good-bye, dear little Hoosh."

13

Niño knew it was a bad place. The switchback of the trail which took it over the divide, from his side to the Canyon Creek side, made a blind turn at the top and, for a distance of a quarter-mile a rider had to go on his other senses, for his eyes were useless. Rock walls rose fifteen and twenty feet on either side of the narrow track leading into and out of the small, boulder-strewn resting spot at the very summit and, within that eagle's nest itself, the wiliest Apache alive might be surprised by the dullest Pima or Papago. The place was choked with scrub brush, bullpines, mountain ash and big rocks. But, if a man could not fly, or leap half a mile, he had to go through "the trap," as his people called it. However, as there was no war on, and certainly no one yet knew that he, Niño, was back in the country, the risk was more in the mind and memory, than an actual one.

He straightened his tired shoulders, sat tall and sure on his panting mount. A man in his place had to fight his fears twenty-four hours a day. And his instincts, as well. With years of hunting each shadow became black when it was only gray, each noise a mountain-slide when it was but a trickle of small stones, and each movement in the brush or rocks ahead . . . or behind . . . or on either side . . . became an ambushed killer when it was simply the flitting of a cactus wren, or the scurry of a pine squirrel.

Yes, the lives of the hunted were hard and dark. But Niño was coming to the end of that dangerous trail at last. Down the other side of the mountain waited Seiber, and the long delayed surrender. It had taken Niño a long time, and the decision to "come in" had been a difficult and weighty one to make. But now that he had made it, and was going to meet its terms with his head high and his heart feeling good within him, he was glad—he was very, very glad. It was like a big stone being lifted from his chest. He felt free again. Felt like the old days. Like the old Niño. Sergeant Niño, F Company, Third Cavalry, USA. The Apache enlisted scout who even the great Tom Horn said was the best tracker in all the West. The sixteen-year-old San Carlos Indian boy whom Al Seiber had made the youngest regular army recruit of his entire race. *That* was the Niño he felt like, now! *That* was the Niño he had made up his mind to be once more—if it cost him his life in the trying.

Just before entering the boulder field at the top, Niño halted his mount and examined the place. But the wind, gusty and strong, was carrying away from him. He could not have heard another horse had there been one coming up the Canyon Creek side, nor could his own pony have gotten the scent of another in such a gale. On the point of dismounting to reconnoiter the top-out on foot, he drew himself up again. Damn! This was no way to be. If he were going to stop and sniff out every rock in the trail he would never get to Seiber. This was an Indian road and the white men seldom used it. Moreover, it was getting late in the day and he wanted to get down the mountain before dark. He clucked to his borrowed mount, pressed with his knees against its side. The Apache mare, rested somewhat by the pause, went forward willingly enough.

At the far side of the rocky bowl, just at the heading of the drop-off into Canyon Creek and the Cañada del Oro, she snorted and flared her ears. Niño's hand dove for the butt of his Winchester but the weapon was only half clear of its underleg scabbard when the white voice, ugly and snarling, burst from the rocks *behind* him.

"Don't try it, Indian! Get down and stand still. I want a better look at that face of yours."

Niño obeyed the order for one reason. It had been delivered, not in English, but in perfectly good Apache. And that fact disconcerted him. When a white man talks your tongue like a brother, you listen. Especially if you know, without turning, that he has a gun aimed at the middle of your back and will blow out your spine as quickly as he will light his next *cigarillo*.

"I hear you," he told his unseen enemy. "I'm waiting."

There was a dry rattle of dislodged rock, then he heard the heavy breathing move close in, and felt the nudge of the rifle barrel between his shoulder blades.

"Turn around."

He turned slowly.

When they saw one another face-to-face, the eyes of both men hardened. Niño recovered first.

"It's a long trail which has no turning," he said, still in Apache.

The other nodded. "You can cut out the Injun-talk, Niño," he answered. "I thought it was you. By God, I'm sure glad I didn't drill you without making sure."

Niño studied him carefully. "Why?" he asked. "What difference does it make?"

"Plenty!" laughed the white man. "For one thing, $5,000 reward. For another, a perfect alibi for me to hand that damn posse of hardrock muckers coming up the hill behind me."

"The reward is for dead or alive," said Niño. "So why didn't you shoot me in the back?"

"Because I want you shot from in front—just like I run into you on the trail, head-on. Then we'll just swap horses, me taking yours and claiming I was coming your way, and then shooting you and putting you acrost the old bonepile I'm riding. Oh, by God, this is the luckiest day of Joe Hare's life. That posse will not only buy my story, but will likely elect me to the Territorial Legislature! And all because of little old Niño!"

"Hare," said Niño, "why don't you shoot? Are you the same coward you were when you murdered that whiskey seller on San Carlos River?"

The white man leered at him, rolling his left eye, which was walled far outward and moved uncontrollably when he was angry or excited. "You dirty red son!" he snarled, "you got no more'n you deserved. If they hadn't of sent you to Yuma for that murder, they'd have sent you for a dozen others you did do!"

"But they sent me for that *one*," said Niño, black eyes glittering. "And all that has come to me since, is because you spread the lie that it was Niño and his *broncos* who did the murder. But for you, my friends would never have killed Sheriff Reynolds and Deputy Holmes on the Kelvin Grade. And, but for you, Niño would still be a sergeant of scouts, with three chevrons and a clean name."

Again Hare laughed. It was a wild laugh, with a bad, crazy sound, and Niño watched him closely.

"All the more reason, you red scut, why I'm going to enjoy packing you in acrost that there old mare I got hid in the rocks yonder. By God, I may even run for governor before this is through. Just imagine, me, Joe Hare, governor of the whole damned Arizony Territory!"

"Why don't you pull the trigger?" said Niño. "You've already got the gun in my belly."

"I'll pull it when I'm good and ready. Meanwhile I want to see you squirm a little. It ain't often a man gets to dangle a $5,000 worm on his hook!"

This was a very good joke and Hare laughed until he had to stop and wipe his walled eye. It was when he did this, the instant and very instant that he removed his left hand from the forearm of the Winchester, that Niño whipped out the skinning knife hidden beneath his red Apache sash.

The steel went in and upward. The terrible wound of its passing from navel to prosternum in less than a heartbeat literally shocked Hare speechless. The other nerve functions went also. He wanted to close his finger on the trigger of his rifle, but it would not answer to the command he sent it to do so. The other fingers would not work either. It felt to Hare as though they were tightening on the rifle's breech, but the weapon was sliding away and falling into the trail dust even as he ordered the hand to close upon its steel frame. He went down into the dust, after it, sagging to his knees as though he were made of slow-running mud, his good eye staring up at the dimming, dark face above him, the walled eye wandering aimlessly off over the mountaintop. When Niño bent to pick up the fallen Winchester, Joe Hare was dead.

14

Many thoughts filled Niño's mind. What should he do about the dead white man? What about his horse? Ought he to take both down to Camp Condon with him, giving them over to Seiber and telling him precisely how it had been that Joe Hare died? Or should he throw the body into some rocky cleft, leaving it for Yosen and the buzzards to deal with? It was not easy to decide.

Finally, he was afraid to do anything with the body of Joe Hare but to hide it. It would be expecting too much, even of Al Seiber, to ask him to explain, not only Niño, but the corpse of a dead white man, as well. Yes, even though it was an evil white man, the miners would not like the idea of Niño—of a dirty Apache—bringing him in across his own horse.

Now as to that horse, that was something else. It was a pretty worthless old packmare, with a shoe gone on the off forefoot and lame in the shoulder because of it. But she could still go, and Niño and Hoosh could use such a pack animal when they moved up to San Carlos and the Chutanay Mesa wickiup, after Seiber straightened out all matters of the law with the money he would get for bringing in Niño. Yes, he would take the old horse along. But Joe Hare must go down into some deep hole in the rocks. That way he would cause no trouble for Seiber, and maybe, too, that way Niño could forget him more easily. When a man has vowed he will kill no more of the enemy, and then he does kill one of them, even though he could not help himself, then it is better to bury the failure and forget it. Yosen would understand, and Seiber and Hoosh would never need to know.

With the decision, he breathed with greater freedom. When he had hidden Joe Hare, puzzling briefly over his ragged Papago attire as he piled the loose stones in atop his soiled body, and after he had mounted-up and ridden the first mile of the down-trail, astride one scrubby mare and leading the other, he was definitely increasing his spirit to its former level.

Perhaps it was because of this relieved feeling that all was well again, that he had not kept his usual wolf-like watch of the way ahead. Again, it may have been the wind, still noisy and blustering down in the canyon. Or, too, it could have been the fading light, very poor now as he drew nearer the creek level, deeper into the shadows of the towering mountain walls. Very probably it was the combination of all these things. Whatever the cause, the result was as sudden as the Joe Hare surprise.

He came out into the bottomland piece of meadow-hay, dry and sear with winter's brown, glad to be free of the steep trail and pleased to see and hear the running water ahead. This would be a fine place to let his horses graze a while and for himself to rest a few hours. There was a dense stand of alders and small pines where the trail went across the stream and up the canyon's far wall. In the twilight, he could just make out the joining trail, which ran down the creek toward the Cañada del Oro diggings.

"Good," he said aloud in Apache to the two mares. "We will rest here. This is sweet hay and clean water. Come on, my friends, one more camp and then tomorrow. . . ."

It was the thought of that last word—tomorrow—which filled his mind, as the mares whickered and lifted their heads in response to his encouragement. But it was a tomorrow which would never come for Niño. The crack of the first rifle was followed by the white smoke of half a dozen more bursting from the dark fringe of the trees at the crossing. The lead whistled and whined past Niño, splattering the rocks behind and about him. His saddlemare reared and the old pack-mare began to pitch. He could not reach his own rifle for his efforts to control them, and, in the instant's confusion, he heard a cry which frightened him more than all the ambush-bullets. It was the voice of Hoosh shouting his name and warning him to turn and flee.

The thought flashed in his mind that they had captured her to use as bait—that they had found out from her about his trip to see Seiber—and had set up this trap to get him as he came off the mountain.

It was a wrong thought. Even as it formed, he saw, through the uncertain twilight, the form of a horse and rider break from the crossing timber and dash toward him. The rider was accompanied by more shots and some bellowed white curses. Then Niño could see both rider and mount clearly; and they were Hoosh and his own gelding, Tobacco; and Hoosh's feet were tied beneath the pony's belly and her hands bound behind her back and Tobacco was running free and on his instinct as an Apache war horse.

"Back! back!" Hoosh was crying in their native tongue. "They are several and they have the canyon blocked both here and across on the other wall! Turn, Niño, turn! I will follow as I am able—"

He was already yanking his mare around. Hoosh was an Aravaipa woman. She saw things the Apache way. There was a time for being brave and a time for running like rabbits. This was a running time. The fact she was a woman and handicapped by her bonds did not enter the situation. If she did not make it free of the meadow, her failure must not bring down Niño also. That was *not* the Apache way. The warrior, the fighter, the man, must live to fight on. The woman was expendable in war. The man was not. Niño was very proud of Hoosh in that moment, but he was striking his old mare with his rifle butt in the same breath.

"Ho! Na-to!" he yelled at Tobacco as the wild-eyed gelding ran past him with Hoosh. *"Ih-yeh, ih-yeh!* keep going, keep going—!" Tobacco flattened his ears and dug into the mountainside with his flinty hooves. The rickety mares were no match for him but under the whip of wind-slapped rifle shots made an honest effort to disprove the fact. The three animals hit the uptrail within a rope's cast of one another. Tobacco, in the lead, took to the incline surefooted as a bighorn sheep. The mares went after him, Niño yelling them on as only an Apache might. Behind, now, the posse men were getting to their tethered mounts and coming on.

A hundred and fifty yards from its bottoming, the cliff trail squeezed between a pair of portal rocks. These granite gatewings were flanked on the in, or mountain side, by thick laurel scrub and on the out, or canyon side, by an eighty-foot drop-off to the rocks of the creek bed below. Niño had marked the place in his guerrilla fighter's memory on the way down. Now, going past the boulders, he slid off his mount, ran back on foot and opened fire on the posse men, just beginning the ascent from the canyon floor.

The latter at once paused to re-assess purposes.

Admittedly the range was long and the light uncertain. Especially for an Indian marksman firing downhill. But the orange-flamed roars of the Apache's 44-40 and the ugly whanging screams with which his bullets splattered the rocks about the advancing miners' committee from Camp Condon, produced some searching second thoughts among the membership at large.

Primary of these was the certainty that an accidental bullet made just as nasty an exit hole as an aimed one. *Ipso facto,* a man could die as fast from lead poisoning in the dark, as in the broad day. Moreover, there had been no bargain struck concerning Indians who would be shooting back. Old "Cochise" Jones, the bearded ex-trooper with Crook in the first Apache War, or anyway the worst, had been the one to think of scouting the creek grove in advance. That had made him the one to stomp out the little squaw and to take her prisoner. Also, it had made him the one to suggest the idea of setting up the dry-gulch for whomsoever she might prove to be waiting for. The figuring here, of course, was that it would be the ragged buck who had run off with the Clark & Scanlon mare. When, in fact, the latter turned out to be the dreaded Niño, the law and order fever had been doused as though with a bucket of cold creekwater. Had not Old Cochise been there to lead the charge out of the timber, there would have been no charge. Not unless it was one back in the other direction. As it was, most of them agreed with what young Mercer had done in knocking aside Cochise's rifle when the old devil had laid its sights squarely twixt the shoulder-wings of the escaping squaw. Not a man there but who wasn't glad he didn't have the death of the pretty little Indian woman on his conscience at that moment. Not a man there, either, who particularly wanted the death of a plug-ugly white man on his mind. Especially if it was his own. It was young Mercer who again set the company tone of live and let live by piling off his horse and hand-leading him back down the creektrail on tip-toe and with tender care to keep the animal between himself and Niño's Winchester. Inside twenty minutes, Cochise Jones was talking to himself in the windy darkness. Directly, he decided he did not care for the lonely sound of the conversation. He, too, departed down the creek, and quietly.

Niño, after waiting half an hour, during which no shot was fired and no sound audible to his keen hearing came up from below, realized that the miners had given up and gone back to their down-canyon camps. He gave the owl-hoot signal and Hoosh answered it from a little way up the trail. Taking the mares, he went up the mountainside and found her waiting in a small pocket on the cliff. Quickly, he freed her of her bonds, helped her off the gelding. Neither of them talked while he massaged the blood back into her numbed limbs. Then, when she could move about, and when the horses had all been tied, they told one another how it had been with them since last meeting.

It didn't make good telling on either side.

Finally, Niño decided that what they should do was to go up to the saddle where Packrat had said to wait for him and Al Seiber. The posse would certainly be back tomorrow and they could not stay on the cliff side where they were. However, it was not far to Packrat's high rendezvous. They could make it easily with a midnight start. Meanwhile, both were bone-weary and the two mares had to have water. The answer would be to sleep until the middle of the night, then go back down below and water the horses before starting the climb to the saddle.

Naturally, there was consideration of crossing over the creek and fleeing through the night, and at once, by the continuance of the old Apache Catalina Road around Tucson and on toward Old Mexico.

The temptation to do this was very strong, too. And very sensible. The Camp Condòn posse would surely alert the whole area to the return of Niño and the Aravaipa squaw he had kidnapped from the San Carlos Reservation. With the five thousand dollar reward still out for him, all the old bounty-hunting Apache-haters would be in the field by tomorrow night. But this course of striking for Sonora by dark had its dangers. With the poor horses they had, they could not hope to cover the seventy-five miles, straightaway, which lay between them and the Mexican border. Not before full daylight. And with that daylight all of the hungry guns from Tucson to Nogales would have clear sighting at them across the barren, shortgrass country of the Sonoita Plateau over which they would be moving by that time.

Countering this certainty, there was the cunning and repeatedly-proved driven wolf's tactic of running a very short circle to lie up in the immediate vicinity of the kill and watch his eager pursuers rush by, pell-mell, on their way to chase him thirty miles into the next county. It was this maneuver which favored Packrat's nearby, but uncharted saddle. From its lofty perch they could see both the Cañada del Oro and the Apache Catalina trails, as well as having the escape route of Packrat's secret short-cut to their immediate rear. In such precarious circumstances as would be theirs with first light tomorrow, the choice of the saddle seemed by all odds the safest stratagem available to them.

Even so, Hoosh wanted to go home to Mexico. Her spirit was bad, she told Niño. It was warning her not to stay in that place. It was saying for her to get out of there. It was seeing dark things, if they stayed. Why couldn't they run for the San Pedro instead of going straight by the Sonoita country? They could sneak up the river just like Niño had done four years ago, to get away from the Kelvin Grade posse. There was a lot of brush and timber and slashed-up hills to hide in, going that way. They could make it easily. She knew they could. The baby would be fine with the grandmother on Aravaipa Creek, until such time as things grew quiet again and they could return for her. Besides, Packrat would be around to look after her, if the old grandmother could not. And, lastly, why trust that Seiber again? Why take a chance on getting killed for him? He wasn't worth it, and he never had been.

"Ih!" she concluded uneasily, "It's no good, Niño. My heart is bad within me. Come on, let's go."

He actually thought about it, then, wavering in his first decision for the saddle and Seiber.

His own heart wasn't right about the thing, either. There was something wrong and dark hovering over the affair. But he was very old at this game and Hoosh was very young at it. She wouldn't know about the shadows that looked like men and were only cactus wrens. Above all, she would not know about Seiber. And about the way that Niño felt toward the big, calm-natured white man.

No, they would stay. They would wait for Seiber.

"Hoh shuh," he told her, "be quiet, Little One. We

will rest, as I have said, then we will go down and water the horses, as I have said. We must be of one mind, Hoosh, and one heart. Else why are we here?"

"*Anh,* yes," she said, and lay down by his side to sleep.

It was three hours later that she awoke with the deep feeling of something having gone amiss. Seeing that Niño still slumbered and hearing nothing either up or down the trail, her fear began to quiet. Then one of the horses snuffled restlessly.

Apache-like, Niño had tethered the mounts between themselves and the most likely approach of the enemy, in this case, downtrail. The idea of this was that the Indian mustangs would give warning of any advance. But the snuffle just now—it had been Tobacco, Hoosh could tell—had not been of the warning variety. Rather, it had been querulous. Or perhaps just curious. But it had not been *just* a snuffle.

Hoosh got up quietly and went down to the picket.

In the heavy gloom she could make out her grandmother's mare lying down at the nearest station, then Tobacco standing beyond her in the second spot. She could not see the Camp Condon mare and thought at first that she also must be down. But she was not. All that was in her place was the piece of frayed tie-rope which she had broken in her instinctive desire to go home. The rope was hanging listlessly from the laurel stub to which Niño had fastened its tie-end, and Hoosh frowned and felt of the ground where the mare had stood. The droppings, when her fingers found them in the dark, were no longer warm to the touch, and the mare had been gone at least two hours and was too far away to even think of going after her. She was an old mare and gentle. She would go straight to her home-corral and be there waiting for her rolled oats or bran with the rise of the sun. There was not even any sense awakening Niño about it, as the miners could not back-track the mare until daylight. The only thing to do was to see that the tie-ropes on Tobacco and the other mare were tight, then go back to bed. The grandmother's mare was much better a mount than the escaped packmare, anyway, and they were actually better off without the latter animal. She might only hold them back in the places that the Indian ponies would get over like goats. But it was when she came to the tie-rope of the grandmother's mare, that her calmness fled.

There was something strange about the way the mare was lying. Her neck was stretched out too straight and there was too much tension in the rope. She would not respond when Hoosh kneed her in the flank to make her get up, and when the tiny squaw reached swiftly down and ran her hand along the distended curve of the furry abdomen, the skin did not switch nor make any move of life.

Moments later, Hoosh was shaking Niño awake.

His mumbled complaints about being disturbed over so minor a matter as the useless old packmare breaking away to go home were cut short by the Aravaipa girl's low-voiced interruption. "It is not the packmare, only, Niño: there is the grandmother's mare, too; she has been shot in the belly where we did not see, and has bled out her life on the ground while we slept!"

Niño said nothing; only sat and stared into the darkness trying to think. But he could think of nothing; nothing save the single grim truth which put the lowness and the urgency in Hoosh's frightened words.

They could not get away to Mexico, or to any place, on one horse.

15

When Wallapai Clark returned next day from Tucson he found Camp Condon celebrating its brush with the famous Apache outlaw. No claim was being worked. But the golden nuggets of hindsight were being mined everywhere up and down the Cañada. By the time he had worked his way up the creek to his own diggings, he had heard eleven versions of the heroic defense of his property, or exactly the number of idle miners who tagged along with him and the silent Scanlon. No man denigrated his own part in the valorous pursuit of the damned renegade and his three—or four—or eight desperate companions. The pretty little Aravaipa squaw was the only element which did not become multiplied, for while a surplus of fighting Indians always worked out fine in the telling, Indian women got in the way and added nothing but possible embarrassment to the tale. So Hoosh stayed single, while Niño became divided more times than the company opinion as to who was *really* to blame for the failure of the creek-crossing ambush.

Wallapai Clark paid little enough heed to this argument.

Unlike Cochise Jones, whose sobriquet was self-bestowed and whose very connection with General George Crook was often suspect, Wallapai had earned his name. He knew Indians and had made a later life-study of this particular Indian. If it had indeed been Niño who cleaned out his cupboard and waltzed off with his three-shoed packmare, he must have been in pretty desperate straits. For a *bronco* of his reputation to risk his life, or even possible identification, for such a poor mount and such scraps of food as he had gotten from the cabin, things would have to be mighty thin with him.

The knowledge kindled a light in his eyes, tightened the muscles over his lean jaws. He didn't yet think it was Niño. But *if* it was, by God, this might finally be the day and place where Wallapai Clark and the ghost of Bill Diehl caught up with the red scavenger.

Of course, these damned fools with him had trampled all sign out of the area around his and Scanlon's shack. He knew that before ever they topped the ore-dump and could see as much, firsthand. What did surprise him, though, and flabbergasted them, was spotting the old Dolly mare standing in the corral with a broken tie-rope dangling from her scrawny neck. That was *something*.

Clark said nothing to the miners of the actual cause of his excitement at seeing the old mare. He waited until they had grown tired repeating their "gospel words" about the " 'Pache attack" of yesterday, and went on back down the creek to ply less knowing ears than his, with the details of their historic ambuscade of "Niño and his twenty desperate Mexican Chiricahuas."

When they had gone, he told Scanlon to leave the packmule loaded and come along. He had a hunch to run out before the light went—it was then late afternoon—and the mule could wait. Scanlon looked at his flushed face and at the bad light in his eyes, and shook his head.

"Reckon I'll stay here," he said. "I ain't lost no Injuns."

His companion's face grew even darker, but he controlled himself.

"I wouldn't ask you," he nodded, "except that, if it *is* him, he may be laying for me, same as I'm laying for him."

"You mean like the way he tried to get at you up to Fish Creek?" asked the big Irishman.

"Like I told you," said Clark, "don't try to be funny. It ain't your jug of cider. You don't want to come along and cover me, I'll get Mercer."

Scanlon glanced down the creek. "Don't look like you'll need to fetch him," he said. "Yonder he comes. Likely wants his dollar."

Clark followed his glance, annoyed. "Well, he can whistle for it!" he snapped. "He ain't getting a dime from me. I wasn't paying him to dip his English pinkies in that damned crick!"

"You know," said Scanlon soberly, "happen you don't get aholdt of that generous streak of yours, you'll die broke. I never did see a man so determined to give away his dust. It rightly puts a lump in my throat."

"It will rightly put one on your damned thick skull," rapped his partner. "You'd best leave off spurring me, or I'll climb your hump. You hear?"

"Sure I hear," shrugged the other. "Hell, I ain't spurring you, Wallapai. You know I ain't got the sense to do that. Nor nothing else halfways bright. I just don't cotton to pot-shooting Injuns. It ain't my speed, like you say."

Clark might have drawn the point out a bit farther, except that young Mercer plodded up just then.

"I say," he chirped in his British accent, "I didn't want to put the teeth on you in front of all those other chaps, but I could use that dollar, Clark, old boy."

"It ain't 'put the teeth,'" said Scanlon patiently, "it's 'put the bite.'"

"Of course, Johnny lad. Jolly good for you. I could use the bloody dollar, none the less."

It was a hot day for February, and Clark was tired from the Tucson ride. His mercurial patience and Scot's ancestry came to a boil together.

"Kid," he said to the pink-cheeked English youth, "you got ten seconds to get over the rise. I ain't funning with you. When I pay a man to watch my place that don't include letting in stray Apaches to stock up on my grub and run off my pack mares. Now you start raising some dust!"

Mercer, no man to debate mining camp morals with an Arizonan—not for a dollar, anyway—took off down the creek as directed. He didn't say a word but Scanlon shifted his chaw and observed that perhaps the Englishman was aware of Clark's well-known fiscal closeness and might be inclined to resent the skinflint treatment at a safer distance. To this Clark replied that he could keep his damned comment to himself, but to go and fetch his Springfield rifle and come along and give him cover up the canyon, while he cut for Apache sign. He didn't really give a hoot whether Scanlon liked it or lumped it about hunting Indians—it was still a damned sight better to hunt them than to get hunted by them. So if he didn't want to wake up later that night with a Cherry Cow buck bending over his bunk with a nine-inch Sonora knife at his Adam's apple, maybe he'd better just let up a bit on the Indian-loving music, and go get his gun.

Scanlon could never stand up to his partner when the latter turned loose, full whip.

He just plain put out the thoughts faster than Scanlon could gather them up.

Besides, it was no joke what he had just hinted about waking up to find an Apache standing alongside your bed. It had happened to many a man in many another lonely camp. There was nothing to keep it from happening on Canyon Creek to John Francis Xavier Scanlon. Nothing better than tough old Wallapai Clark, leastways.

"Sure," he said, gulping dryly. "I was only joshing you right along. You knowed that, Wallapai. Shucks—"

"Get the gun," said Wallapai Clark. "And shut up."

The Clark & Scanlon claim was the last but two, and those abandoned, above Camp Condon. The canyon bellied out above the diggings, the creek running through an extensive flat of small pine, juniper and giant artemesia sage. The men of the camp, used to Arizona's mineral-belt dryness and scantness of tree growth, called it "the forest," but it was scarcely that. Beyond the "forest," however, the sides of the mountain closed in once more, narrowing to the gorge at the upper crossing of the Apache Trail. It was extremely rugged past the crossing, the creek heading higher up in the jumble of slides and rockfalls which nothing less than antlered game or mountain cats might negotiate. The most prominent of these rock-faces was the enormous collapsed shoulder, or the fork, really, of the high saddle where Packrat had set the rendezvous. This great cascading mass of stone had a fan, or footing, of perhaps 500 feet in height, upon which grew a fringing of coniferous scrub. Above this steep skirt, the scarred and broken baserock of the mountain itself rose almost vertically to the tree of the saddle. It appeared to be, and had been assumed by a generation of white prospectors to be, unscalable. From creekfloor to saddle seat, the elevation varied 900 feet. The miners of the Cañada del Oro had a name for it, of course and, with the poetic practicality of rough, untutored men, it was a literal and a good one—Scar Face.

It was beneath this looming drop that spread the nearly level fan of Jackpine Flat, the name some unimpressed California Sierra men had bestowed upon "the forest." And it was here that Wallapai Clark spent the waning hours of daylight searching for undisturbed sign of his enemy. He found none and, by the time he had worked up to the crossing, the light was poor indeed. When he had come as far up the cliff trail as the portal rocks, he was down on hands and knees straining to see. Scanlon, watching the rocks, the laurel thicket and the trail above, shrugged and lowered his old Springfield, satisfied that the hunt was over and that not even Wallapai Clark could read sign in such light.

He was wrong.

"By God!" the latter cried, coming to his feet, "here

it is! One track. One damned set of moccasin prints and that's it, you hear? He *was* alone and it *is* him. God knows I studied that trackline of his long enough—the left foot toed-in more than the right; the right run over on the heel and pushed extra deep on the inside ball of the big toe!—Scanlon, it's him!"

Somehow John Scanlon wasn't glad to hear it. He had hoped it wouldn't be the poor devil. He had never seen Niño, other than the brief flash of him scuttling through the gray dawn at the Fish Creek ambush, and he was not, as Clark accused him of being, an Indian-lover. You didn't live and work in the Arizona Territory of the Eighties and Nineties and come off with any overwhelming affection for the Apaches. Not hunting pay-color you didn't. From the days of old Ed Schieffelin and his silver strike that started Tombstone, the Apaches had been the main hazard for a hardrock man in those parts. At this same time, Scanlon was an Irishman, and his Gaelic soul rebelled at any warfare pushed home by great numbers of outsiders against a tiny brave band of original inhabitants. He understood perfectly well that O'Tooles, Moriaritys, Flanagans and Delahantys were passing scarce among the Chiricahuas, Mescaleros, Gilas and San Carlos. But he was damned if he didn't admire the terrier spunk and wild free spirit of the red spalpeens, and damned if he was going to let Wallapai Clark, or any other man, talk him out of it.

"Faith! you're a wonder," he said to Wallapai. "What a shame it's got dark on you. I'd have liked to seen you crawling up the cliff on your pewbones."

The other man was too stirred up to argue the point.

"Listen," he said, "there's blood here, where he stopped and fired back. It's gut-shot blood; dark and clotty."

"It don't mean nothing. Might have been the little Injun lady, God forbid, or one of the horses." Scanlon turned downtrail. "You can stand here licking your lips all night if you've a mind to," he told Clark. "I'm going back to the shack."

"So am I," agreed his companion quickly. "Just as fast as I can leg it."

There was a new excitement in his voice, and Scanlon eyed him suspiciously. "Why for?" he said. "What's the sudden rush? You can't do nothing till morning."

"Oh, can't I?!" said Wallapai Clark, and picked up his swinging walk to a near-trot of nervous, hunting-animal urgency.

16

When Seiber and Packrat came into Camp Condon it was sometime after ten o'clock that night. Since it was socially *de trop* in Old Arizona to enter with an Apache Indian into the unwarned presence of good honest white citizens, the former left his pudgy companion in the high brush beyond the first camplight, going on, alone.

Down at the single canvas-and-log saloon the sourmash was flowing like creekwater—at one silver dollar the shot. Easing in without drawing undue attention, Seiber got his elbows on the bar and bent an educated ear.

The talk was mainly of the big Apache raid of the day previous. Increased by twenty-four hours and half a keg of Old Crow, the story had grown as by the mathematical progression of the lone penny multiplied endlessly by itself. Yet Seiber was even older at the game of dividing such nonprofessional reports by ten, or a hundred-and-ten, than was Wallapai Clark. He had not finished his first drink before he knew precisely what the situation was, or rather what it *had to be*.

Still, he did not hurry because of the certainty of his hunch. He might still learn something of use, and it did not occur to him that time, short of sunrise, was of any pressing importance. Once he had learned that darkness of the day before had let Niño and Hoosh get cleanly away up the cliff trail, and that Wallapai Clark had been in Tucson and only returned this same afternoon, late, he relaxed. It was his thought to go out, directly, pick up Packrat, circle the camp, head up for the rendezvous at the Saddle. Once there, they could rouse up Niño and the girl and move out, by Packrat's secret short cut, for San Carlos. By daybreak they would be a long way gone and, once back on the reservation, a safe surrender could be arranged at Packrat's *rancheria.* One thing, meanwhile, was a certainty. The temper of an Indian-scared mining camp was not the one to which to expose a famous *bronco* bent on giving himself up peacefully to the law. Not, for absolutely sure, a mining camp containing the hot-headed likes of Wallapai Clark.

No, he decided, the way to play this was by ear.

In the process of so doing, soaking up misinformation, whiskey fumes and cigarsmoke in equal proportions, he was belatedly recognized. This was along about eleven, when the retired Indian expert, Cochise Jones, came in for his accustomed try at trading one of his moth-eaten lies for a free nightcap. Introduced by Cochise, who stood to shine in the reflected light at least another five years, Seiber knew he was trapped for an additional half hour, at the best. It would never do, now, to depart with any sign of unnatural haste. Once recognized, and under the circumstances of Niño being in the vicinity and Clark sworn to go after him with first tracking light tomorrow, he had to move very carefully. His friendship for the Apache and his less than love for Wallapai Clark were scarcely any secrets to these grizzled ore-dump gophers. Taken together with his surprise appearance in Camp Condon, late at night and covered an inch-thick with trail dust, they comprised a suspicious set of coincidences, Seiber knew. To prevent them becoming anything more concrete, he played up to Cochise's deathgrip champeronage with all the stomach he could muster, meanwhile searching desperately for a safe way out.

It was eleven-thirty before he found it. At that time, the young Englishman, Mercer, alone and quiet at the end of the bar for over an hour, suddenly moved up to Seiber. He had not appeared drunk but now he took the big German's arm, linked his own in it, murmured, *"Come on, I'm stone sober,"* and broke into a maudlin, weaving chorus of *"God Save the Queen."*

Caught short, but with a mind used to spot decisions, Seiber lifted his glass and joined in. They marched, thus, twice around the tiny room and out the low-beamed door, the scout's bass voice and the boy's tenor, convincing the most interested critic that (1) they would never make any money as a duet and (2) that both would realize the fact after baying at the moon and getting a bite of the night air.

The truth was not quite so simple.

Outside, Mercer dropped the charade, pulled his powerful companion into the shadows alongside the *cantina.*

"My friend," he opened, "I think I have something to tell you."

Seiber eyed him cautiously. "You're the English kid Clark hired to watch his place," he said.

"Indeed," answered the other. "Employed but not compensated."

"Uh-huh. Well, whatever that means, I fail to see what it's got to do with me."

"You may be right, old chap, but I've gathered the idea you would like to find that Indian rascal before Clark does. Of course, if I've misguessed your intentions—"

"Maybe you have, maybe you haven't. What you got?"

"Well, this afternoon, after Clark chased me off his

bloody property, I stole back and spied on him. I had a notion to pilfer his blooming billet, when he went down to the camp. You know, lift a pound of coffee, bag of sugar, some little thing—get my pay one way or the other, damn it all."

"Sure. Then what?"

"He didn't go down to the camp. Cheeky beggar didn't even unpack the poor mule. Left the brute standing under full load, while he and Scanlon took their rifles and dashed off up the creek. I rather fancy that suggests something to you, eh what, old boy? I mean, under the beastly circumstances and all?"

Seiber's broad jaw jutted grimly.

"Johnny Bull," he said in his quiet way, "you are damned correct it does. Let's ramble."

Circling back, they picked up Packrat, rode cautiously up the dark side of the diggings past the last of the shacklights of the camp-proper. Turning the bend of the creek, they let the horses out, went the mile to Mercer's claim at a sharp jogtrot. Beyond that, they slowed, as Seiber did not care to come in on Wallapai too precipitously, or without politic and appropriate notice. Starting up the rise toward the cabin, he raised his voice in a popular gold-camp version of *"The Girl I Left Behind Me."* It wasn't good, as the man said, but it was from the brisket. It ought to have brought the dead above ground, too, but it did not. They got clear up to the front door and still no sight nor sound of Wallapai Clark.

But, then, listening intently, they caught a jumbled monologue from around in back, and, seeking it out, found John Scanlon and the slim remains of a stone jug of Taos Lightning in the pole corral communing with the packmule.

The old mare, Dolly, was nowhere to be seen, and Seiber's quick search of the cabin showed that structure empty, with no signs, even, of supper having been set earlier. Back at the corral, it became increasingly evident that Scanlon had drunk his meal, as he was so limp he could not stand upright, and so thick of tongue and full of half-audible Gaelic complaints that he couldn't, or wouldn't, recognize Seiber, much less reply to his questions about Wallapai Clark. Adding to the confusion, both Scanlon's and Clark's saddle horses were in their shed-roof stalls at the far end of corral, as were both of their saddles and bridles. Clark had taken the old mare out on a hand-lead, that much was apparent. But why? And where? And how long ago?

These things Seiber *had* to know.

He picked up Scanlon and threw him boldily into the horse tank at the near end of the corral. The tank was filled with a ditch taken off upstream from the creek, and the February snow water was cold enough to turn a polar bear blue. Scanlon gasped, cried out in wild alarm, strangled, cursed, pawed for solid support. When he found it—the rolled rim of the sheet-iron stock tank—Seiber cracked his knuckles with the butt of his rifle, shoved him back under, held him there. Directly, he hauled him out, hung him over the fence to drain. By the time the Irishman had found his breath, and the strength to fall off the top rail into the corral droppings, he was talking sense.

He had sought the solace of the stone jug because of the cowardly failure to speak up like a man with his partner, he said. As for being discovered in company with the mule, that, too, was Clark's doing. The latter had so often directed him to seek the brute's society, that, tonight, when he had wanted to unburden himself of his shame, he had just naturally come out to tell it to Samson.

Seiber shook him up at this point, saying that all he wanted to know was the whereabouts of Wallapai Clark and the missing packmare. Scanlon replied that this was the very cause of his present condition, and that he would never get over his guilt for not having stopped Wallapai when he could. Seiber looked uneasily at Packrat, tightened his grip on Scanlon's collar.

"You drunken flannelmouth," he said to him very

softly, "where has Wallapai gone with that mare, and what's he up to with her?"

"Seiber, lad," said the other, shivering with the cold and the wrack of the drink, "it's what I'm trying to tell you, with apologies for myself. He's gone to bait that poor heathen Injun with Old Dolly. Claimed that once an Apache's laid halter to a horse, he won't let it get away from him. Said he would bet his bottom dollar Niño would follow down to get the mare back soon's he figured it was safe. I don't know nothing about Injuns, but I don't cotton to shooting them over no set-baits. 'Specially when there's squaws around. Anyways, we had a hell of a row over it, but I turnt yellow and backed down. It sure was the Lord's blessing I had the jug hid and the mule to talk to."

Seiber had let him get it all out, not wanting to break in for fear of confusing him. Now he let his feet back down to the ground, releasing his grip on his icy collar.

"I'm not blaming you none, John," he said, "but I'll tell you something you can do for that Indian if you want to make up for not laying it on Wallapai, and that's to guide me up to where he's apt to be with that mare. You got any definite ideas on that?"

"Hell, only one place he could be, 'less he changed his mind. That's a pot hole clearing about a mile due up the crick. On the flats yonder. Little meadow called Rifle Springs. Only real piece of mountain hay hereabouts. Wallapai figured it'd be the natural place for the mare to stop on the way home—or figured the Injun would think so."

"He meant to tie her out and set a gun over her?"

"Sure. Said he'd make her tie-rope look like it had snagged and hung up in some brush of itself. Then lay up and wait all night. Figured he'd have himself a Injun 'fore daylight. Maybe two. Said I could tell by how many times his rifle cracked."

Packrat, who had stood by silent as a rock, nodded his bullet head. "His rifle might not be the only one you can count tonight," he said, and levered his Winchester. "Come on, Seiber, *schichobe,* let's go."

"All right, we will. John—" He took Scanlon by the arm, led him off four or five paces, continued quietly. "I want to ask you a favor. If anything happens up there tonight, you ain't seen nor talked to neither me nor this here Indian with me. What do you say?"

Scanlon eyed him uncertainly.

"You meaning to cut down on Wallapai?" he asked.

"No, only get to him before he cuts down on Niño."

"You still want the Injun alive, Seiber? On that crazy deal you made him about the reward money?"

"Yes I do, John. And I want your hand on it, too."

The Irishman nodded, stuck out his rock-hard fist.

"You've got it, then," he said, "and damned glad I am to give it to you. Good luck." He glanced suddenly over toward Mercer. "Say, what about the kid yonder?" He'll talk sure."

"I don't think so," said Seiber. "I heard in the bar that he knocked aside old Cochise Jones' gun up there at the crossing. Saved the squaw's life, likely. That don't sound like an Apache-hater to me."

"Well, maybe not. All the same—"

Seiber interrupted him with a quick wave. "All right, I'll call him over." He signalled the young Englishman to come up and, when he had, put his huge hand on his shoulder. "We got a gentleman's agreement, Scanlon and me, to say nothing about me and this here Apache of mine passing this way tonight. We both take it that you'd be of the same mind. Are we right or wrong?"

"You mean you want me to keep my bloody mouth shut?"

"No, I just want your hand, here and now, that you never saw me after leaving that saloon yonder."

"What do you intend doing, old chap?"

"I'm going to try to keep Wallapai Clark from killing Niño, or that young girl he's got with him. There may be trouble. I won't ask for it and I won't walk around it."

"Bully for you. Here." He held out his slender hand. "By the Lord Harry, I'm happy to be aboard. Shove off, chaps. But, I say—," he added sharply, "—no sitting shots, you know; you must take him on the blooming rise!"

Seiber issued his first and last smile of the night. It was brief, and gone as quick as the glint of the moonlight from his strong white teeth. Reaching in his pocket, he spun a silver dollar toward young Mercer, who automatically caught it. "There's your pay for watching Wallapai's place," he said tersely. "In case he don't come back, I don't want to see you cheated."

Mercer grinned, tossed back the dollar. "I'll return it if you don't mind," he said. "I've heard about you and your balmy offer to spend the five thousand defending this Indian in the courts. Count me in on the case."

Packrat moved in with the horses.

"Schichobe," he said to Seiber, "remember that they found the grandmother's mare dead on the cliff trail yesterday. Remember that I said we would be at the meeting place with sundown of this day just past. Remember what you know of the restless way Niño is. We'd better go."

Seiber frowned, nodding quickly.

Packrat was right. In the saloon stories he had picked out certain hard facts. Of these, the main one was that the miners, going back up the creek crossing and cliff trail the morning after missing Niño at the ambush—which would be this past morning—had discovered the dead Apache pony just beyond the Portal Rocks. With the escape of Wallapai's packmare, this had to mean that Niño and Hoosh were down to one horse. Add to that the fact that he and Packrat had missed the sunset rendezvous and you came up with a conclusion that Wallapai Clark had figured the situation with deadly knowledge of the Indian character and that Packrat was meaning to imply as much by his present guttural warning.

He took his horse from the Apache, swung up on him.

"There's no missing this Rifle Springs meadow?" he asked Scanlon.

"Nope. You go right up the crick. You'll hit Jack-pine Flat 'bout a mile from here. Meadow opens out on your right 'bout another mile crost the flat. You can check it by looking off your left shoulder, and up. You ought to see a hell of a rock-face going up sheer beyond the pines. Scar Face, we call it. The trail cuts over the crickside quarter of the clearing. Out toward center there's a jumble of good-size rocks and brush. That's likely where Wallapai will be laid up."

Seiber heeled his horse around.

"I hope we've understood one another," he said to Scanlon and Mercer. "In case we ain't, I'll be back."

Before either could reply by word, or even wave, of acknowledgment, Seiber and the squat Apache were gone. Watching them lope swiftly through the moon-light, down the cabin rise and toward the rocky trail along Canyon Creek, Scanlon shook his shaggy head.

"Faith," he said, shivering not from the chill of the horse-tank alone, "and I hope we have too."

"What's that, Johnny lad?" asked Mercer.

"Understood each other," replied the Irishman. "Sure and I think I'd rather have that Niño on me neck, than Al Seiber."

"Why," said the young Englishman, "I thought he was an excellent fellow. Completely charming. Wonder-fully interesting chap."

"It depends," said John Scanlon, still shaking his head.

"On what, old bean?"

Scanlon took a last look off through the daybright glare of the Arizona moonlight.

"On what you think of two-hundred-pound white Apaches," he said.

The night lay winter-still. Wallapai Clark looked at

the moon and the shift of the high stars, and guessed the time to be midnight. He moved his legs and arms, working them to restore the cramped circulation. He had tied out the mare at eight o'clock, had been lain up in the rocks beyond her since that hour. It was cold in Rifle Springs meadow. Frost was beginning to form from the dew on the sear old hay of the clearing. Wallapai blew on his fingers, massaged those of his trigger-hand with the others. The steel of the Winchester was so chilled that it tended to stick to his moistened fingers. Damn! why didn't Niño come!

He ought to have shown before this. He would have come down into the canyon with the first darkness, trailed down it toward the diggings no later than nine o'clock. But, then, he would have been working afoot, and so might have required considerably longer than nine to get as far down as Jackpine Flat. It all depended upon how far away he had been laid up during the day. Wallapai had a strong hunch it had not been far, but you never knew with Apaches. Niño might, actually, be on his way to Mexico, and a hundred miles gone by now. Yet the posse had killed his horse and if Wallapai knew Indians, he wouldn't let a thing like that go unavenged. The Apaches worked it on an eye-for-an-eye basis always; so it was logical to assume that in this case it would be a horse-for-a-horse. Or, at least it *had been* logical so to assume. Now, Wallapai was not so sure. And it was almighty cold in that clearing.

He would give it another fifteen minutes and go home.

He began to count underbreath. By five minutes his hands were getting numb again. He put down the rifle, blew on them, started the second count. Ten minutes. And nothing moved in the meadow. Thirteen. Fourteen. Fifteen.

Wallapai started to roll over and sit up.

Out in the open, the Dolly mare, dozing where he had snagged her broken tie-rope over a gnarled juniper limb, raised her head and blew out through her nostrils.

Wallapai froze.

The mare's ears were pointed creekward, and now she snuffled again and whickered low in her throat. There was something over there in the shadows of the stream-brush.

Moving an inch a minute, Wallapai eased back over on his stomach and got his Winchester to shoulder. Nothing happened. The mare put her head back down and went to sleep again. But Wallapai did not move a muscle. He knew Apache Indians better than his old packmare did. He held in his breath so that its vapor would not rise into the moonlight over the rocks and betray his presence. He cursed the cold and the numbness which crept through his shooting hand because of it. But he did not move. Nor did he take his eyes from the stream-brush.

The ten minutes which crawled by were each an hour long. Any man but Wallapai Clark, or another with a hatred to match his, would have given up. And would have missed the slight movement of the shadow stirring now across the pin-still clearing.

At first it was only the indistinct shape of a human head reared above the creekside cover. Then the head arose to reveal shoulders. Then an upper body. And, finally, the full figure, creeping forward toward the mare. Wallapai squinted to clear his straining vision, then cursed and set his teeth. But he did not ease his finger on the trigger simply because it was a woman's figure coming toward the mare.

They always did this, damn their red souls to hell. Always sent their squaws out first. They knew, the red sons, that the Army had issued orders to all troops, and requests to all civilians, to refrain from shooting Indian women. Since the order, the Apaches had made full use of it, too, even though the sending out of the women was an old custom practised long before any Americans were in the country. Well, orders were orders and requests were requests. But not in Jackpine Flat or Rifle Springs.

With the thought, Wallapai's sights steadied on the squaw. But his finger did not close on the trigger. Out of the creek shadows a second figure was now stealing, and this one was not a woman. Wallapai's heart turned over. His jaw muscles clamped so hard they ached. He knew that slight form. That wiry, bow-legged, slender, long-haired silhouette. All right, Bill Diehl! here comes your time! I told you I'd get him for you, and there he comes, sharp and black as any target bull's-eye in this god-blessed bright moonlight! Now—

But it was not to be now.

In the moment his finger curled around the curve of the trigger, the second Indian moved into a line directly behind the first, who was now at the mare's tie-rope.

And worse.

The woman was straightening up with a smothered Apache warning that the mare's rope was tethered to the limb—tied by hand and not snagged by chance—and Wallapai could hear the Indian words as clearly as the crouching brave behind the tiny woman.

"*Ih,* Niño! a trap, the mare is the bait! Run! run—!"

Wallapai shot her as he would have shot Niño in her place; with a vicious curse and with black anger. She crumpled and fell, clearing the sightline at her companion. As the latter wheeled and raced, bent double, back toward the shelter of the creek timber, Wallapai fired three aimed shots at the zig-zagging figure. Twice he knocked it down, once on the first shot and again on the third. But each time it leaped and staggered lurchingly to its feet and drove on. When it was gone into the blackness of the stream-brush, Wallapai lowered his rifle and waited several minutes before he came warily to his feet.

Even then, he did not go near the tethered pack-mare, nor the huddled silent figure upon the ground next to her. Neither did he make any pretense at following up the wounded second Indian. If it were Niño, and Clark *knew* that it *was,* the squaw could be as deadly a bait for him, Wallapai, as the mare had been for the Apache couple.

It was shortly before twelve forty-five that Wallapai Clark went out of Rifle Springs meadow on the far side. It was a quarter of one when Al Seiber and Packrat came into it on the near, creek, side. They went on the run to the tethered mare and the small, pitiful figure on the ground beside her. Seiber bent quickly and placed his hand beneath the still-warm left breast. He stood up after a long, long moment, and nodded wordlessly to Packrat.

They had missed their rendezvous with Niño; but little Hoosh had not missed hers with Yosen.

The trail was not hard to follow. Niño's wound, one of them, anyway, was situated and of such a nature that its discharge of blood ran down the left leg, soaked the moccasin, spilled over it to leave, with each tortured step the trademark print of Niño's toed-in left foot stamped upon the steepening rocks of the creekbank. The moon, glaring down with paper whiteness, let them run the bloody track almost at the trot. Half an hour brought them to the base of Scar Face. Here, Niño had lain on the rocks to rest. Seiber knelt and felt the blood. It was fresh and sweet to the smell. "Ten minutes ago," he said to Packrat. "Maybe five."

The Apache went to one knee alongside him, placed his own fingers to the spot, sniffed them critically. "Five," he said. "We must hurry. There's enough blood here to fill a canteen."

They went on up, unable to believe that the crippled Niño had been able to drag himself where they had trouble following in full health. Another half an hour of slower going brought them to the top of the 500-foot baseslide of the great monolith's skirt. Above them, fifty yards, the rubble and the piled rock of the centuries ended. Beyond, and rearing over them, the sheer 400-foot face of the giant rock shone ghostly white and spider-shadowed by its thousand-year pattern of wind and water erosion.

The two trackers paused, studying the way ahead.

It was Packrat who broke the stillness.

"He's up there," he said. "He has to be up there."

Seiber nodded. "I figure in those split ledges where the slide peaks. Right?"

"Yes. In that deep cup of shadows directly above us."

Seiber nodded again. "There's a powerful lot of shooting moonlight between us and that cup. How you reckon we ought to work it?"

Packrat frowned, shaking his head. "I really don't know, *schichobe*. He's a crazy Indian since Chuana died. Now little Hoosh has been killed too. I think he might shoot us as quick as he would Wallapai. Me, anyway." He paused, adding thoughtfully, "But you, Seiber, I don't have a true idea what he would do with you."

"You mean I'd have a better chance of getting to him than you would?"

"I think so, yes."

"You think we ought to give him the owl hoot first?"

"No, never. That's the way Wallapai nearly got him at Fish Creek. There's no chance to signal him. It would only give him an aiming place."

"Suppose I yell up at him? My God, he certainly knows my voice, bad hurt or not."

"Yes, I agree. But knowing your voice and knowing you mean to help him, ah, those are two different matters. As he is now, crazy with the wound and the anger and the fear of Wallapai, and with the heart-sickness over Hoosh, I don't know what he would do. He might let you come up part way, and shoot you when he had you close enough not to miss. I think that's the way we must reason, Seiber. Yes, right now he would kill even you."

Seiber shook his head. "But, damn it, Packrat, you just said you thought I'd have a better chance with him than you would. What kind of a chance are you giving me, walking up there to be shot in the face? Thanks, but I'll pass."

"No, I meant you would have a better chance with him if you could get to him. He might listen to you, I mean."

"Yes, that's so, he might. *If I can get to him.*"

"*Quien sabe, amigo?*" shrugged Packrat. "These are the odds of life. He may already be dead up there. I will go if you are afraid." He started to get up, but Seiber pushed him down, and hard.

"I will let you know," he said, "when I need any fat Apaches to be doing my dirty wash for me. Besides, one of us has got to go back and bring up the horses. I nominate you. Get going."

Packrat patted his shoulder quickly. "All right. I'll meet you at the foot of the slide in one hour. *Cuidado*—"

"*Cuidado* yourself," said Seiber, getting his feet under him. "You make any racket getting below and start that poor bled-out devil to whanging away at me, up here, I'll track you till you're a hundred-and-ten years old. Now you better believe it, *hombre*."

"*Ya lo creo,*" answered Packrat soberly, "I believe it," and disappeared silently down the moonlit slide.

Seiber waited until he was well gone, then went forward up the near-vertical assent to Niño's suspected last *querencia*, his final hiding place.

It took him thirty minutes, half of Packrat's allotted hour, to get to the jagged teeth of the ledges behind which he expected to find the desperate outlaw. These upright, narrow rocks, implanted in the manner of a devil's postpile in the broken detritus of the slide, were fifteen feet high. At first inspection, Seiber could see no way over or around them. Then he noted the smear of black blood directly in front of him, and saw where a twisting track no wider than a big man's thigh, went upward through the postpile. How he managed to squeeze his bearlike hulk through this snake's crevice, he never knew. He only knew that he did, and that it brought him out onto the rimmed ledge of decomposed rock and windblown soil caught in the saucer of the "cup" he and Packrat had studied from below. In that saucer, face down, small body hunched up and harmless as a broken doll's, lay the dark-skinned San Carlos youth who was wanted, dead or alive, by the Territory of Arizona, and whose head, brought in a burlap bag to any Army post from Yuma on the Colorado to Fort Bayard in New Mexico, was worth $5,000, gold.

Seiber stood at the rim, looking down at him.

In the moment's hesitation, all the bitterness and frustration and anger of the years he had fought for this Indian boy's life, flooded up in him. Everthing he had risked and gambled and bet on the chance that he could find him alive and well, could persuade him to surrender and come in and stand his trial, once for all, was lost and gone and blown away as the sands of the Mojave.

There he was, the terrible outlaw Niño, lying in the dirt, huddled and lonely and forlorn, no bigger than a half-grown white boy, and no more dangerous now. There he was, the legend and the lie and the last of the fighting Apaches in Old Arizona. There he was, Sergeant Niño, Company F, Indian Scouts, Third U.S. Cavalry. Seiber's friend. And small blood brother. Waiting for him in the still, quiet moonlight. Peaceful and calm and unafraid.

Stone-cold dead on the mountainside.

17

It was late now, Packrat would be waiting below. If he went now, he and the little Apache could be cleanly out of the country by daylight. But Seiber was not going to go without Niño. He owed his former scout that much.

Crossing the small shelf, he picked up the slight form, put it as gently over his shoulder as though life were yet in it. He got back down through the postpile rocks the same way he had come up through them, because he had to do it and not because it was a practical, or even possible thing to do. Even so, and though the way was tortuous, his twenty years in that land of danger made his every move an instinctive one to hide his passage. The nature of the slide, almost continuous rock, abetted the unconscious care. When he had gotten down to Packrat and the horses there was no appreciable sign left on the mountain, except Niño's original blood-stained trail up to the "cup."

But at the horses the situation changed.

There the ground was partly dirt and would hold the prints of their mounts, and of their own moccasins. The latter sign, especially, would be bad to leave in the vicinity. Niño was too famous to be allowed the courtesy of an ordinary disappearance. The hue and cry after him, when the Camp Condon posse ran into the dead end at Scar Face slide, would be long and loud. Any "extra" sets of moccasin prints at the base of that slide might be followed up with embarrassing, if not dangerous, results. Packrat, thinking of this, called out to

Seiber as the latter approached the end of the rock and was about to step onto the bordering canyon floor.

"*Schichobe,* wait, I will bring up the ponies a little closer. You can hand up Niño to me and get on your horse from the rocks. All right?"

Seiber understood at once the need for the suggestion. "Yes, all right," he said. "Come on, there's a piece of shelfrock here just saddle-high."

Packrat brought the big German's horse up, his sad hound's face drooping, tiny eyes beading with bright tears in the moonlight. "Is he *dah-eh-sah?*" he asked, reaching to take Niño's body.

"Yes," said Seiber, bending to hand down the slack form. "Have you got him?"

Packrat held Niño in his arms as he would a sleeping child. "Yes," he replied, "I have him. Take your horse and let us go from this evil place."

Seiber swung down into the saddle, gathering his reins. At once, Packrat touched his arm. "Wait," he said, "Niño is without his headband. Did you see it on the slide going up? It's a red one."

Seiber frowned. "No, there wasn't anything going up. Damn! It must have fallen off up in the cup. I never thought to look."

"That's bad, *schichobe*. It gives them some sign to keep excited about. It would be better if they found nothing. I imagine you scraped out his footprints and your own up there?"

"Yes, I did. And I was careful coming back down. But we can't go back for the headband."

"I'll go," said Packrat. "It will not take me half an hour. Maybe less."

"We may not have half an hour," objected Seiber. "You can't fool around with Wallapai Clark. You know that."

"Indeed, *schichobe.* But Niño is dead. What more harm can Wallapai Clark do to him? Or to us, for that matter?"

"That isn't the idea. I don't want them to have his

body, nor the satisfaction of seeing him dead, nor of letting that damned Wallapai crow that he killed him. Now do you?"

"No, *schichobe,* forgive me. Let's go."

Seiber clucked to his horse, began guiding the animal down the slope to the creek bank trail. Packrat followed with Niño. After they had gotten on the trail and were moving up it toward its junction with the old Apache Catalinas road, Seiber spoke again.

"Do you know a good place to put him to sleep?" he asked Packrat. "The sooner we hide him, the better. I'd like to have it done and us gone, come daybreak."

Packrat rode a moment before replying. Then he shook his head. "Seiber," he said, "I don't understand you."

"Neither do I," said the big scout bluntly.

"No," insisted the other, "I mean it. Here you are with this small poor body that is worth five thousand dollars if you ride in with it to Fort Lowell or Fort Huachuca tomorrow morning. The body is dead. It feels nothing anymore. It isn't anything except a dead body of a dirty murdering Apache. I don't understand you. You would bury five thousand dollars just to keep Wallapai Clark from knowing he killed his enemy? You, a white man? It's crazy."

Seiber thought a moment, his broad face clouded.

"Packrat, you know damned well I've thought about that five thousand. Any man alive would do that. But we're talking about a friend; about Niño; about a boy that I raised up and gave his first chance and made the finest scout of that ever sat a saddle in the U.S. Cavalry. I got a lot of years yet to live with myself, even if Niño's dead and gone. What good is the money going to do me, played off against the idea of me bringing in my best friend dead over a horse? I wouldn't do it, *schichobe,* for five million dollars. And it ain't because I'm pure as mare's milk, neither. I ain't no more noble than the next son trying to make a living and keep out of jail doing it. But this boy was like my own kid. Bringing him in and selling his body would be like—well, I don't know—it just don't seem natural nor decent. Nor it don't seem fair neither. Niño fought his whole life to be something, to amount to more than just another poor damned Apache Indian. I figure the least we can do is see he dies the way he wanted to live—decent and with respect from his friends, both red and white. Now I grant you that burying five thousand dollars just so an Indian kid from San Carlos can rest easy in his grave, ain't far from what you said. But I been called crazy by half the sane people in the territory, so adding you to the list won't topple me over. Now, you know a place to put him, or don't you?"

Packrat only nodded, speaking very quietly. "Yes, a fine place and not far; come on."

Seiber nodded in return. "Here," he said, reaching over for Niño's body, "better let me take him, so's you can take the lead. We're going to be short on time."

On the point of surrendering his friend, Packrat hesitated, a peculiar expression forming on his homely features.

"Seiber," he said slowly, "how long do you think he's been dead?"

The big scout shook his head. "An hour maybe. Why?"

"He's still warm. He doesn't cool. Feel him."

"Don't be a fool!" Seiber was short with it. "You know a body doesn't cool out that fast. Of course he's still warm. Now hand him over and move out."

"No," said Packrat, "I mean *very* warm, Seiber. Put your hand on his."

"Damn it," said Al Seiber, "an Indian is always an Indian. You got more imagination than an old maid. You—"

He cut it off sharply, tightening his grip on the limp, slender hand of Packrat's burden. That hand *was* warm. It was too warm. And dry-warm. Not clammy, nor puttylike.

Seiber pulled in his horse.

"*Hold up*," he said tersely to Packrat.

The last witness to see Niño in or near the Cañada del Oro was never brought to testify. Perhaps it was as well. Like "Comanche," the sole Seventh Cavalry survivor of Yellowhair's heroes at the Little Big Horn, "Tobacco" would probably have refused to cooperate. Horses are that way.

It was growing gray in the east when Niño's gelding, twelve hours tied and very restive, raised his slender head and blew out through his nostrils in the quick, sharp mustang way.

There were two horses coming up the last steep rise of the great cliff, into the windswept, cloud-high seat of the saddle above Old Scar Face; two horses, but three riders. Tobacco stomped nervously, pricked his small ears, stretched his muzzle to catch the information on the light breeze coming to him from the travelers. He received both white and Apache scents, and was confused. The next moment, however, the riders drew near enough and he recognized the small fat one coming alone in the front. It was the same one who had come with him and the little squaw to this saddle two suns before. At still closer sight, he had a feeling of familiarity, also, for the great, broad figure of the white man riding second. The one with the other Apache asleep in his arms, carried like a child close to his breast and carefully held. Then the riders were up to him and he had the full scent of them, and he was whickering and stomping and pawing in his eagerness to reach out and nuzzle the still figure in the white man's arms.

"Look at him," said Packrat, "he knows him; even this way he knows it is Niño! A great horse, *schichobe*. One of the very best. *Ho, Na-to! Shuh, shuh!* be quiet. He is here. We have brought him back for you."

Seiber didn't answer, only waited wearily for the small brave to get down and relieve him of Niño's motionless form. When the latter had done so, he climbed down stiffly, flexing and slapping his paralyzed arms. It was ten minutes before he could close his fingers, twenty before he could use them sufficiently to loosen the cinch-buckle of his girth and slide the saddle off his rawboned gelding. By that time Packrat had the fire going, his rusty coffee-tin retrieved from his hiding place, filled at the spring which bubbled from a rock basin nearby, placed on a forked stick over the crackling flames and beginning to hiss and simmer. When, next moment, he brought forth from the camp cache a half bag of Arbuckle's best blend, together with a hand-grinder, Seiber was ready to kiss him. The aroma which arose in the following minutes from the blackened sheet-tin container, called a coffee pot by Packrat but a "FEED MEASURE, U.S. ARMY, 1 QT." according to the legend embossed across its sooted bottom, was heady enough to arouse the dead. Or the dying. Or even the merely unconscious and deeply asleep from exhaustion.

On his bed of Army blankets warmly placed beyond the fire and in the shelter of the rocks which shielded the campside, Niño stirred, sighed heavily, tried to raise himself. Seiber was by his side at once, pressing him back.

"Rest easy, *schichobe,*" he told him. "We are here with you, Packrat and Seiber, your old friends."

Niño was too weak to reply, but he understood and moved his head slightly to indicate that he did. As yet, his eyes were not even open, but Seiber, feeling for his pulse and finding it strong and even in its rhythm, looked up and nodded to Packrat that all was well. The chubby brave wiped his nose on his sleeve, nodded back, turned away as though it could not matter less. Yet, when he had produced a piece of good bacon from the cache and had it sliced and broiling in thick chunks over the breakfast flames, he was whistling a very distant version of Seiber's, and the Third Cavalry's, favorite melody, *"Tenting Tonight"*; and the burly German scout had to hide his grin and amused headshake. It wasn't, actually, the fact that Packrat was such a poor whistler, nor even his unlikely Apache's choice of a white man's old Civil War tune to practice on, which warmed Al Seiber's heart. What got to the latter, and deeply, was the typically Indian fact that, in all his years of scouting and friendship with the pudgy San Carlos, he had never known him to whistle a note, good or bad. Now, to hear him chirping away like a tame magpie, taken in company with the odors of fresh-ground coffee and broiling bacon, was surely an omen to be reckoned with. When, a moment later, he felt Niño stir again beneath his hand, and looked down to see the slender youth's eyes were open and unclouded, Seiber knew that feeling of rare *rightness,* which may come no more than once or twice in any man's life.

He put his thick arm beneath the thin shoulders, raising his friend so that he might see the fire and smell the good warm food and drink preparing over it. Also, so that he might see, and feel, the snug safeness of the place to which he had been brought. Packrat, noting the movement, came over and squatted on the other side of the blanket-bed, smiling a little awkwardly at Niño, the way a man will do with a very sick brother.

"Packrat, dear friend . . . and Seiber . . ." Niño's voice fell away with weakness, and they waited for him to recover. "How am I to thank you?" he went on, after a bit. "What is there I may say to you both, who are my only friends . . . ?"

With the hesitant words, he put out his hands, the right to Seiber and the left to Packrat. Each man took the offered member, holding it in both his.

"You just said it," Al Seiber told him, and tightened his grip.

Niño nodded, waited another while. "Hoosh," he said at last, "she is *dah-eh-sah?*"

"Yes." It was Seiber again. "I don't think she even knew it. A clean head shot."

"*Anh,*" muttered Packrat, "Yosen guided it, Niño."

"*Anh,*" replied the other. "I knew it; I could tell by

the way she went down. Did you leave her there, *schichobes?*"

"We had to," said Packrat. "But I am going back for her, Niño. I will find her and take her home, wherever they have put her. You have my word for it. If you live or if you die, Hoosh will not be left among these strangers."

Niño moved his head in thanks. He looked up at Seiber, then, trying to smile. "Well, *Jefe,*" he said, "that brings us to me—to the great Niño. What do you say? How bad is it? I can't tell yet. I seem to feel nothing."

Seiber patted his hand.

"It's bad," he admitted. "How bad, I don't know. You took one across the scalp, which is no worry and already crusted over. The other one is through the meat of your left ham, and it hit a bloodline in there. You must have lost half what's in you. We got it stopped down below, though, and she didn't open up again coming up the hill. That's something."

Niño lay back upon the blankets. "And if it opens up again," he said, "what then?"

Seiber's face tightened. "You know," he said.

"You will take me away, *schichobe?* You will not leave me in a strange land, among strangers?"

"Yes, old friend, I'll take you away. They will never find you. But I will mark the place, and Packrat will know where it is, and he will pass it on in trust when he grows old. You won't be forgotten. Niño. Your own people will know where you are, always."

He had spoken the vow in Apache, in order to be sure that Niño understood it as a blood-brother promise. Now the latter moved his head slightly, his voice very low.

"And how will you mark the place?" he asked.

"As it should be marked," answered Seiber in strong English: "*Sergeant Niño, Company F, Apache Indian Scouts, Third Cavalry, USA.*"

He saw the smile pass faintly over the graying lips, felt the slight figure relax peacefully beneath his hand.

He looked quickly at Packrat, then bent and put his ear to the thin youth's breast. When he raised his head again, his eyes were dark with apprehension.

"Is he asleep once more," asked Packrat, "or is it the other thing at last?"

Seiber only shook his head, and pulled up the blanket.

"I don't know," he said.

Epilogue

The posse from Camp Condon, led by Wallapai Clark, found Niño's blood-soaked headband in the cup at the head of the slide below Scar Face. And that is all it ever found of him. Although no discernible trail led away from the cup, Clark searched for days before abandoning the possibility his victim might be alive in nearby hiding. After that, he never relinquished the conviction that his two ambushing shots had, indeed, killed the famed *bronco;* that Niño, mortally wounded, had crawled into some remote rockhole and there died. Most Arizonans of the time tended to agree. Not even Apaches, they said, were able to vanish into thin air. And they confidently predicted that one day the bones of this one would be found, precisely as Wallapai claimed, in some arcane crevice or rattlesnake cave off the flanks of Old Scar Face.

Two disparate miners from the Cañada del Oro diggings did not share this assurance, but neither did they deny it. John Scanlon and the English boy, Mercer, honored their handshake with Al Seiber to the very last. From that night of the moonlight ambush at Rifle Springs, Niño was not seen again in Arizona. Wallapai Clark went contentedly to his grave, certain he had avenged the death of William Diehl, and not in his lifetime, nor since, has any reliable eye-witness come forward to deny the old man's insistence.

Oh, there were pretenders. Colonel Kosterlitsky of the Mexican Rurales stated in 1899 that Niño was known to be ranching with some other American

Apaches (presumably Massai's band) in the Mexican Sierra Madre. But the Colonel didn't see Niño, and neither did any of his men. They only *heard* about him.

So did many others hear of him. For twenty years Arizona cowboys were manufacturing tall versions of having run across Niño out on the range—but it was always so far out on the range that no corroborating witness could possibly have been present. A few U.S. Cavalry officers entered claimers of having brushed with the vanished one in the field, also. In the resulting heroic chases, of course, the patrols almost, but never quite, came up to the quarry. Which is as it ought to be.

Niño became, and he remains, a legend of the land and time. Did he live? Did he die? Was he alive and well in Old Mexico long after that dark day in Cañada del Oro? Did Seiber and Packrat get him safely away? Did they leave him in some lonely mountain crypt high in the arid desolation of the Santa Catalinas? *Quien sabe,* as they say in that country. Al Seiber never talked. Neither did Na-chay-go-tah, the fat bachelor packrat of Chutanay Mesa. There is but one thing absolutely certain about the fate of Niño, and that is this: he is the only hostile Indian ever to have successfully defied the U.S. Government's full armed forces in the field, and to have disappeared in the end as completely and bafflingly as he had done so repeatedly and easily in the years when he was being harried and driven by every ambitious lieutenant, hungry sheriff and scrofulous bounty hunter in the territories.

Later in that last year of 1894, the Legislature's standing $5,000 reward was withdrawn and the long hunt for Niño came to its official end. But only to its *official* end.

There were certainly three men who might have had something pertinent to enter into the record book before it was closed. One of these was a fat San Carlos Apache who came forward to claim the body of the young Aravaipa woman, Hoosh. This was at Camp

Condon ten days after the ambush on Jackpine Flat. The brave was questioned, of course, but would say only that the girl was a cousin on his mother's side. He produced, as well, a note from the dead woman's grandmother indicating she was next-of-kin and requesting that the body be given over to the bearer of the note. The latter document was witnessed and countersigned by the agent at San Carlos, and so was honored. The body was exhumed from its shallow bed of piled rocks near Rifle Springs and hoisted roughly into the mule-drawn farm wagon which the San Carlos brave had driven, the good Lord knows how, up the Cañada to Camp Condon.

The other two men who might have had more to say than they did, were also San Carlos Apaches; two cavalry scouts sent over with the investigating patrols from Fort Thomas and Fort Apache. The scouts were good ones and managed to do what Wallapai Clark had not—picked up the track of the two horses at the foot of the Scar Face slide and run it out to its dizzy topping on the high saddle above. But there, at the campsite found among sheltering big boulders, they seemed suddenly and inexplicably at a loss to go farther.

The horse sign about the camping spot, they said, was at least one week old, and the human sign—what might have been the telltale marks of soft-tanned Apache *n'deh b'keh* moccasins—had all been nicely brushed away with pine branchlets.

What was that? Oh, yes, surely there had been *someone* camped there. But how many, *quien sabe?* The scouts could only say there had been three horses, all shod, two with American-type shoes, one with Mexican. Indian horses? White men's horses? Honest horses? Stolen horses? Who, indeed, could say? Not the two scouts, that was plain. All they could guarantee was that whoever had been there, had been there on or about the day Wallapai Clark shot the two Apaches over the old packmare, had stayed there about three days after that, and then gone away on their horses into the untrackable rocks on the San Carlos side of the summit.

Well, now, actually, there had been one other certainty, one other clear sign left by the departed campers. But neither of the San Carlos scouts thought to mention it to their officers at the time, or to any white man at any time thereafter.

It did get rumored around, though, among the Apaches over on the Rio San Carlos, the Gila, and down along Aravaipa Creek. What the sign was, the reservation story went, was a good clean moccasin print over behind the fireside rocks. It was where one of the campers had "stepped deep," apparently in the process of lifting a considerable burden. This was alongside the sign of the Mexican-shod horse, as though the burden might have been deposited across its back, or, better yet, in its saddle. In either event, the moccasin print was a fine one, and rather unusual, too. It was half again as broad, and two times as long, as that of any *n'deh b'keh* ever worn by an Apache. Also of interest was its odd impression, run over on the outside and twisted a little, the way, say, that a right foot would make its mark, if the left foot were injured or crippled in some way. As to who it might be who would wear such a moccasin big enough and broad enough for a grizzly bear, and who might also be known to be crippled or hurt in the left foot, the two San Carlos trackers could not imagine. But they feared that someone else might do so, given the opportunity. So they simply looked at one another, exchanged thoughtful nods, glanced over at the officers and men of their patrols, saw that no one was watching them at the moment, thereupon, and with quiet, complete skill, scrubbed out the solitary huge footprint with their own moccasins.

After this, the tale concludes, the scouts went over behind another rock and lifted their canteens in a twin toast to the departed. The creekwater in the canteens contained a liberal lacing of green-mash *tulapai*. With another aimless hour of prowling the campsite for sign, the two canteens were empty, the two scouts full, the two officers commanding fed up. The senior captain ordered the arrest of the scouts and the retreat of the combined patrols to Camp Condon. His name, whatever it might have been, has been lost to posterity—perhaps deliberately. But the bright-eyed oldsters down on the San Carlos will still reveal to a politely inquiring visitor the names of the two Apache scouts. And will furnish a very wise, happily wrinkled grin to go with them. They were Kai-ra-nih and Espinosas, sometimes known as "Josh" and "Nosey."

So ends the Indian story, and the Apaches say the true story, of the darkfaced San Carlos youth whose father called him Red Wolf, whose few forgotten friends called him Niño, whose many remembered enemies called him mad dog and murderer, and whose name in the hundred legends and one thousand lies since told about its bearer, has come to rest on history's tongue with yet a fourth and far more famous sound.

It is Apache Kid.

Henry Wilson Allen wrote under both the **Clay Fisher** and **Will Henry** bylines and was a five-time winner of the Golden Spur Award from the Western Writers of America. Under both bylines he is well known for the historical aspects of his Western fiction. He was born in Kansas City, Missouri. His early work was in short subject departments with various Hollywood studios and he was working at MGM when his first Western novel, *No Survivors* (1950), was published. While numerous Western authors before Allen provided sympathetic and intelligent portraits of Indian characters, Allen from the start set out to characterize Indians in such a way as to make their viewpoints an integral part of his stories. *Red Blizzard* (1951) was his first Western novel under the Clay Fisher byline and remains one of his best. Some of Allen's images of Indians are of the romantic variety, to be sure, but his theme often is the failure of the American frontier experience and the romance is used to treat his tragic themes with sympathy and humanity. On the whole, the Will Henry novels tend to be based more deeply in actual historical events, whereas in the Clay Fisher titles he was more intent on a story filled with action that moves rapidly. However, this dichotomy can be misleading, since *MacKenna's Gold* (1963), a Will Henry Western about gold seekers, reads much as one of the finest Clay Fisher titles, *The Tall Men* (1954). Both of these novels also served as the basis for memorable Western motion pictures. Allen was always experimental and *The Day Fort Larking Fell* (1968) is an excellent example of a comedic Western, a tradition as old as Mark Twain and as recent as some of the novels by P.A. Bechko. At his best, he was a gripping teller of stories peopled with interesting characters true to the time and to the land.